I0594291

CAPRICORN

EDITED BY AUSTIN P. SHEEHAN,
JOCELYN SPARK & ALANAH ANDREWS

THE ZODIAC SERIES

The Zodiac Series is a collection of twelve speculative fiction anthologies, each focusing on one of the Zodiac signs. The anthologies feature short stories and poems inspired by each sign, and retellings of the various myths behind those signs.

Capricorn Aquarius Pisces
Aries Taurus Gemini
Cancer Leo Virgo
Libra Scorpio Sagittarius

The Zodiac Series has been produced by Aussie Speculative Fiction, and each anthology contains a diverse selection of tales by talented writers from Australia and New Zealand.

I AM CAPRICORN

Zoey Xolton

I am the sea-goat and my constellation is Capricornus.
My tarot card is The Devil; I am a natural born leader
and strategist.
At my best I am hard-working, determined and
disciplined.
At my worst I am condescending, pessimistic and
unforgiving.
Strong and stable, like my element: Earth, mine is a
Cardinal sign.
I appreciate family, loyalty, tradition and music.
At times, I hate all things.
I am ruled by Saturn, and am guardian to the sixth
day of the week.
My colours are brown and grey.

About the Author:

Zoey Xolton is an Australian Speculative Fiction writer,
primarily of Dark Fantasy, Paranormal Romance, and Horror.
Her works have appeared in over one-hundred themed
anthologies, with more due for publication!
She has recently celebrated the release of her debut short story
collection Darkly Ever After. *You can find further details*
regarding her many publications on her
website: www.zoeyxolton.com!

CONTENTS:

FOREWORD

Sasha Hanton

Capricorn or Capricornus is the tenth sign of the Zodiac. Represented by a goat or fish-tailed goat (sea-goat), the name Capricornus fittingly translates from Latin to mean "goat-horned". Ruled by the planet Saturn; named after the Roman god of time, wealth, and agriculture whose Greek counterpart was Chronos.

The mythology of Capricorn can be traced back to ancient Sumer, and the Sumerian god of fresh water, mischief, and wisdom Enki/Ea. On Babylonian monuments, Enki is depicted as a goat-fish. According to some sources Enki and Ea are the same god, but either way both are portrayed with horns and a fish-tail. Ea is usually referred to as a god of magic and wisdom and Babylonian myths of Ea tell of him rising from the ocean to teach humanity the wisdom of the gods.

Of course, the mythology behind Capricorn does not stop in Sumer. As with many constellations, Capricorn holds ties to Greek mythology. The constellation of Capricorn has three different myths that are believed to be related to it. The first and most commonly known is the myth of the goat (or in some cases a goat-tending nymph) Amalthea who tends to the god Zeus when he is a baby, letting him suckle goat's milk. After defeating the Titans it is said Zeus placed Amalthea in the stars as thanks, hence the constellation Capricorn was born. Other figures of Greek mythology considered to be connected to the constellation are Pan, Aegipan (goat-pan), and Pricus, father of sea-goats.

This star sign is also connected to the Devil card in the Major Arcana of Tarot. In Tarot, the card of the Devil is often shown with a depiction of Baphomet, a goat-headed demon with the wings of a bat. It is a card often misunderstood and viewed as bad or restricting with its depiction of the Lovers in chains, but when you look closely, the chains are actually rather loose and could easily be slipped. Divinatory meanings behind this card in its upright position involve domination, violence, black magic, and a bondage to the material. However, in the reversed position it is a card of spiritual understanding, indecision, and the start of physical healing. Capricorn is linked to this particular tarot card because of the tendency for people born under this star sign to strive for the best, and their nature to feel restricted and limited by expectations. However, as with the chains in the card, these restrictions can easily be slipped off if a Capricorn seeks to remove them. Many people view the depiction on the fifteenth card of the Major Arcana as a link to Pan, which gives it another connection to Capricorn.

Limitations and restrictions are part and parcel of Capricorn's inner struggle, ruled by Saturn—the planet of limitations and structure. Saturn is considered to be the planet of constriction, the task master of celestial bodies, and it is because of this planet that Capricorns are said to be determined, hardworking, and disciplined.

The constellation of Capricorn itself is referred to as the Gate of Death; it is one of two constellations viewed as a Gate of the Gods, along with the constellation of Cancer. It is said that, after death, souls ascend to the heavens and travel through Capricorn, the Gate of Death, before returning through Cancer, the Gate of Men.

For those born between December 22nd and January 19th, this is their Sun Sign. Capricorns are known for being ambitious—climbing their way to success in the same way as a goat climbs a mountain—and are often viewed as the business people of the Zodiac. Other traits associated with Capricorn are being realistic, sensitive, persistent, and practical.

For a serious sign with a practical drive for success, there are many darker aspects associated with it as well. As you read through this anthology you are sure to find many different elements connected with Capricorn.

About the Author:

Sasha Hanton grew up in the tropics of Darwin, Northern Territory. From a young age, she devoured books and iced coffee, both of which she continues to intake on an almost daily basis. Now living on beautiful Bribie Island in Queensland, her time is split between writing and spoiling her puppy Miley.

Sasha, who has a Bachelor of Journalism from Bond University, has dabbled in the journalistic profession but finds fiction far more fascinating. Her first published work The Short Story Press Collection *draws on her love for a diverse range of genres and passion for short stories. Coming from a multicultural background (Eurasian) she aspires to make her writing inclusive for people from all walks of life and to bring a unique blend of eastern and western culture to her writing.*

Throughout her life, she has been a lover of history and mythology, and at any time will find some way to worm one or the other into her storytelling. When she's not writing or reading she can be found walking her dog and volunteering. You can keep up with her writing over on www.theshortstorypress.wordpress.com

THE SEA FATHER'S DUE

Nikky Lee

I run across the sand, phone stretched at arm's length, trying to keep the video frame on Mitch. Mitch runs ahead, skipping over seaweed and the washed up driftwood brought in by last night's storm.

"You see that, Nate?" he shouts, pointing at a large clump lying on the tideline—just like we rehearsed. I zoom in with the camera, pixellating the mysterious clump, but it's enough to make out the shape. Dry scales glint orange and pink in the evening light.

"Whoa!" Mitch grabs a stick—we planted it there earlier—and pokes the corpse. I pull the zoom back and hurry over.

It's a fish tail, a marlin according to Mitch. He should know, he and his Dad go fishing every other weekend. The smell of it hits the back of my throat as he comes close. It's everything I can do not to gag—and that's just the tail. The torso and head is worse. The goat had been long dried out in the summer sun before old Hodge let me have it.

"For crab pots," I'd said. And the goat farmer had shrugged and pointed to the fly-ridden body lying in the tray of his Ute.

"Knock yourself out."

And crab pots had been the plan, until the marlin washed up. Then Mitch had one of his ideas.

I zoom in on our goat-fish monstrosity as Mitch pokes it.

"What the hell is it?" he asks, circling.

"You got me." I cringe as the words come out louder than intended. I pace behind Mitch, slip-sliding in the sand, careful not to let the camera land on the twine we used to sew our gruesome creation together. If I shoot it from *this* angle—I step to one side—it's almost convincing. Almost.

Who are we kidding? No one will believe this for a heartbeat.

But I keep filming. My phone is old, scratched and beat up from years of use, but it's better than Mitch's, so I'm on camera duty. Mitch is the better actor too. My best friend's face morphs through the expressions we agreed upon: open-mouthed wonder, wrinkled-nose disgust, furrowed confusion, and he grows more confident with each mask he dons.

When we're sure we've got everything we need, I flick the phone off. "Done." I put a hand over my nose. "Now get rid of it before I barf."

"No way, we might still need it," Mitch insists.

My eyes are watering. God the smell is bad, like I've stuck my head in compost. I try to breathe through my mouth, but its pungency slicks on my tongue and when I swallow, I taste rotten fish. The thought of carrying our goat-marlin corpse back up the beach makes the bile rise in my throat.

"I'm not putting that back in my car," I tell him. Once was bad enough. Never again. "Ditch it or you're walking home."

Mitch purses his lips, scrunches his nose and huffs. "All right. Help me throw it out."

Together we grab our sea-goat, one hand on hair, one on scales, and lift it between us. The marlin's tail is wet and sticky under our palms as we sling it into the surf. It bobs there a moment, the goat's hollow eyes and dry nostrils bubbling, white hairs of its pelt swirling across the surface, before a wave crashes over it, tosses it through the green room, and sucks it down.

We inspect the footage inside my sun-spotted Corolla. The video shakes something chronic, but a bit of wobble adds authenticity we reason. Besides, it means viewers can't look too closely, can't see the slap-dash way we've strung the goat-fish thing together.

"How long will you need to load it?" Mitch asks when we pull up to our rental—a two-bedroom place with peeling painted weatherboard. More of a shack, really, but it's the best we can afford.

"Give it an hour," I say.

Mitch gives me half before he's hovering over my shoulder again. He checks his own phone and our YouTube account.

"Still not there," he says.

"Really? I hadn't noticed."

Mitch gets the hint. He scowls between his locks of salt-crusted hair and leaves me to it. I connect my phone to the charger, the loading bar on the screen a quarter full, and turn on the TV.

Hours later when I check the video, it has had no hits. *What else had we expected?* And now my car smells like fish and dead goat.

I sigh and go to bed.

"Nate, look! We're famous!" Mitch barges into my room in nothing but his boxers, and thrusts a phone under my nose. A video plays through the cracked screen. Our video. I glance to the view count.

"Two hundred and sixty thousand views," Mitch trumpets. "Buzzfeed picked it up overnight."

I blink, forcing my sleep-addled brain to focus. This is big. This is progress. I sit up. "You're sure?"

"Yes, look." Mitch taps the screen and turns it back to me. There's a still shot from our video on display, and beneath it, a short article. The headline reads:

Boys Butcher Bodies for Hoax

My stomach folds. This is not how it was supposed to go. I snatch Mitch's phone and scroll to the comments.

Lawkli | 11 minutes ago
This is disgusting.

ObnoxiousPanda | 14 minutes ago
You sick fucks.

Nick H. | 15 minutes ago
Seriously? I mean really, who do they think is going to fall for this shit? I can SEE the string.

The rest of the 243 comments are much the same. I hand Mitch back the phone, my stomach turning tight. Do police arrest people over this sort of thing? The animals were already dead, but . . .

"We should take it down," I say.

"No way, it's just getting traction."

"Mitch! No one believes it. They're tearing us a new one. We look like idiots."

"So what? Famous, infamous." Mitch shrugs. "A view is still a view. Once we set up video ads, the cash will trickle in."

I'm not so convinced. But Mitch persuades me to leave it up for another day. After all, what's done is done. And we got fifteen hundred subscribers out of it. People are interested. Or perhaps just morbidly curious. At worst, YouTube will take it down. If not, well, perhaps there's a few bucks to be made.

"Ride the wave," Mitch says, "see where it takes us. Just for a little while."

I snort and get ready for work, pulling on an oil splatted uniform with *Murray's Fish and Chips* embroidered on the pocket. Just before I leave, my phone buzzes. It's Emma.

We need to talk about the video. Call me.

My mood sours. Great. A scolding is coming, and I can imagine how it will go. My girlfriend's voice will start soft, deadly even: *What the actual fuck, Nathan? What were you thinking? Did Mitch put you up to this? Another one of his get-rich-quick schemes?* Then it will grow louder as she gains momentum: *He's full of shit, Nate. Seriously, why do you put up with him? You're better than this.* And so on and so fast I won't be able to get a word in.

My phone lights up in my hand. Emma, ever impatient, has decided to call instead. I shove the phone into my bag and let it ring out.

It happens that evening. I head to Beacon Bay after work as usual and pull up beside Mitch's wagon. Compared to my hatchback, it's a tank of a car and he drives like it is one too. The rims are scuffed and there's a dent in his back bumper. The fuel light is permanently on—I've never known Mitch to fill up the tank.

Mitch is out on the grass waxing his surfboard, hand running in loving circles over the fibreglass, sun-kissed face serene. Over the dune, the waves are small, churning over at knee height. Not great, but I don't care. Even if the sea was millpond smooth, I'd still go in to get the film of grease and smell of deep-fried batter off.

"Catch you down there," Mitch says, grinning as I strip down to my undies and wrestle one leg into my wetsuit. I nod and he hurries off across the dune, board tucked under an arm, stride long and eager for the water.

A minute later I'm following, tugging the zip of my wetsuit up as I go. We've got the beach to ourselves—Beacon Bay is too far from town for most locals to bother with, and certainly too far for tourists. Not that we get all that many, not out here in the middle of woop-woop.

Seaweed and debris are still scattered across the sand, waiting for another high tide to drag it back to the ocean, or pitch it higher up the beach. Mitch is already in the water, paddling through the white foam toward the breakers. If I hurry, I'll catch him before he does his first run. I'm the stronger surfer, my long arms carry me further with less effort. I splash into the shallows and the surf surges around my legs. A strong undertow urges me deeper, pulls at my ankles and behind my knees.

Odd.

Beacon Bay isn't known for its undertow. The slope of the beach is too gentle to generate much force from the backwash as the waves surge up the sand, then race back to the sea. My gut knows before I do. It curdles inside, clumping tight like spoiled milk.

A yell—more a splutter than scream—rips across the water. Mitch. He's at the breakers, bobbing up the face of an unbroken wave, kicking at the water. Fighting. He floats to the crest of the wave—and his head jerks under. His fingers scrabble on his board for purchase. Then the scene drops behind the wave and out of sight.

"Mitch!"

I should get on my board and help him. But I don't—can't—move. The water pulls at my legs.

The next wave comes. Mitch's head splits the face and he rises with it, coughing, hair webbed across his face. He scrambles onto his board, knees under him, and digs at the water, paddling as hard as he can. His mouth hangs open, bottom lip trembling as he gazes into the water. A keening reaches me. He's sobbing. No, *begging*. The wave moves under him and I see what he's trying to do. His board pitches on the crest, teetering, ready to plunge down the face of the wave and carry him away from whatever lurks beneath.

And he stalls. It's as if he's caught on the end of a rope; a fish at the end of a line. He buoys on the crest, going nowhere. His face is pale and afraid, and one hand reaches for the shore—for me. He makes no sound, but he mouths the unmistakable word: "Help!"

Standing dumb in the shallows, I see, or think I see, water trickling *up* his arms. But that's impossible. I blink and shake my head, then lose Mitch behind the wave again.

And when the wave passes, he is gone. No scream. No gurgle. Just gone.

I search the water, hunting for a shape, a sign. There's nothing but the foam and hiss of churned seaweed.

"Oh God," the words come in a croak. "Oh God."

Something grabs my leg. I feel it through my wetsuit: a cold, firm grip that wraps around my calf. I yell and leap backward, scattering spray. For a horrible heartbeat, the grip holds, tethering me in place, and its pressure washes up my legs, tightening around my thighs, my hips and groin.

Panic obliterates all my control. I scream and kick, dropping my board to the water. The grip on my legs eases and whatever it is under the waves probes the fibreglass. Water crawls over it, tendrils of wet slopping over the wax. I turn and run for the beach.

The swell nips at my heels, clawing and slipping down my legs. But I'm shallower now, more of me is out of the water than in. The grip can't hold. I hit the sand and keep running, imagining the wave following me up the beach, a great monster of salt and seaweed rising out of the blue to chase me down and pull me back in.

I collapse above the tide line. Sand sticks to my hands and legs. Soft, warm, dry. Panting, I roll onto my side and stare at the sea. The next set of waves rolls in, breaking along Beacon Bay's reef. Snatches of pink and orange glints off its peaks, catching the spray in a rainbow. Perfectly normal. Beautiful even, and for the first time, terrifying.

Bile rushes up my throat and I puke right there on the beach.

The media's calling it a shark attack. But I know better as I sit in the police station, waiting for them to take my statement. The coast guard was out for hours, outboards chopping the length of Beacon Bay. Divers searched the reef. No sign of Mitch. No shark at all, not one—which is unusual.

"Not even a Wobbegong hiding in the rocks," crackles the report over Constable Horgan's receiver.

"Thanks Ann," Horgan responds, clicks the receiver off and rubs a hand over his grey moustache, and I know he's trying to buy himself time to think.

"I'm sorry," he says, after a long pause. "But it's been twenty-four hours. I have to call it off."

I nod, unable to think of anything to say.

Horgan slumps behind his desk, sweat ringing the neck and armpits of his uniform. He pulls his keyboard over and dusts a stray hair off it. "Tell me again what you saw."

It's been a long day—well, night and day—since I called triple zero, half crazed, babbling about the sea. The operator thought I was off my face on weed. I told him I wasn't. He didn't believe me. I clear my throat. Perhaps I should lie, but what should I say?

Constable Horgan coughs, impatient. I'm out of time.

"The water got him," I say, then mumble, "that's what it looked like."

Horgan's eyebrows slump into a frown; his moustache bristles as his lips purse. It's the same story I told him last night. "Nothing else?" His face softens. "Look, I know you don't want to think about it, but it's important we're sure—"

"Sure of what? That he's dead?" I blurt, and my stomach shrivels because the words suddenly make it real.

Mitch is gone. Dead. Oh God. The last look on his face flashes into my mind, fear sapping his cheeks, mouthing that word to me on the beach. *Help.* My fists clench. Don't think. But my brain betrays me and it plays the moment again.

"Here." Horgan pushes a mug of hot water into my hand. I jump; I hadn't even heard him move. "Tea or coffee?" he asks, holding up a jar of instant and an English Breakfast teabag.

"Coffee."

He scoops the granules out and drops them into my mug. Water slops over the side, scalding my wrist. I don't react. Instead, I let the water sting my skin. Let it burn. In my head, Mitch vanishes behind the wave. I should've done something. Should've tried to save him.

"Now, are you sure you didn't see anything?" Horgan asks again. "We need to make sure there's no danger to the public."

My hands shake. More water slops to the floor. So that's what this is. He doesn't care about Mitch. Mitch is already dead, there's nothing he can do about that. No, Horgan's concern is for the public's safety. I understand his logic, but that doesn't stop the rage from simmering in my gut. I put the mug down on the table before I spill any more.

"It wasn't a shark." My voice is firm. "There was no blood. He wasn't eaten."

Horgan rubs his chin again and his eyes narrow, almost

imperceptibly, but I notice and my gut flutters.

He doesn't think I—

On the edge of the table, my coffee cup slips and falls. With a crack and a tinkling of china, it shatters. Coffee splatters across the tiles.

Horgan swears and hauls himself up, jabbing a finger at my chair. "Stay there. I'll find a mop." He shuffles off and I hear him banging about in a cupboard down the hall. I sink into myself, staring at the black puddle pooling out from my smashed cup, but not seeing. I'm back on the beach again with the water clawing at my legs. Mitch is gazing at me, tears in his eyes, face drained of its colour. He knew then. And I'd just stood there and watched.

Coward.

A finger of luke-warm heat brushes my ankle. I blink and look down. The coffee puddle has reached my shoes, soaking the soles of my sneakers. With a 'tch' I lift my feet. They come away from the floor tacky, like I've stood in gum.

And then I see it. A string of black water slips up from the ankle of my sock. It wiggles up my leg, tickling the hairs as it inches higher—like a roach.

I yelp and brush it off—a deft flick of the hand, a move usually reserved for spiders—and scramble up on top of the chair.

The coffee puddle ripples.

One watery arm runs across the floor. It stretches towards me, like a sightless, black amoeba probing its surrounds. The arm reaches the chair leg and the rest of the puddle catches up, pooling at the base of the chair. Then the puddle begins to run *up* the chair leg.

Nope. Nope, nope, nope. The memory of that cold hand gripping my calf jolts my heart into my throat. *It can't be.*

A sliver of puddle trickles over the edge of the plastic seat, beelining for me. I ease back on the chair. *Don't let it touch you,* something inside me whispers, old and primal. The water trickles to my shoes, quicker than before. It's getting confident. *Stronger.* My skin prickles.

Fuck this.

I turn and leap, clearing the chair and the puddle with a good metre to spare. There's a flicker of pride in me as I do it, just a small one. I was a school track champion once, hurdles were my specialty. Muscle memory and all that.

My shoes hit the floor and I bolt. Out the door, down the corridor, into the foyer.

"Hey!" Horgan calls after me and takes up pursuit. "Nathan!"

Don't stop. Don't look. It's after you.

Something in the ceiling groans, the pressure of it shudders overhead, a rusted squeal, like the turn of an old tap. I sprint for the station entrance, passing a drink fountain jerking and jostling in its wall brackets. *Oh God, it's in the pipes.*

I throw myself against the door, utter a whimper of relief as it swings open, and dart into the car park. Emma is waiting in the car, scrolling through her phone. She jumps as I thump into the driver-side door and try the handle.

"Fucking unlock it!" I scream at her.

"Steady on, I'm getting to it." She leans across and pulls the tab up. I scramble in and fumble the keys out of my pocket.

"What's the rush?" Emma asks. Her eyes narrow, and they flick to the police station. "What did you do?"

"Christ, nothing, all right?!" I jam the key into the ignition and turn. My Corolla, ever reliable, hums to life and I throw it into reverse, then back into first as I pull out and zoom onto the main road.

Emma watches me the whole ride home. Her hazel eyes study me from the passenger seat, sliding from my heaving chest to sweat-slicked neck, then up to my white-knuckled grip around the steering wheel. When I pull into the driveway of our—my—rental, her expression is steely.

"What's going on, Nathan?"

"I—" I swallow. "I don't know." *Where to even start?* "I really don't." And this is true. Because it doesn't make sense. None of it makes sense. I'm going crazy. Shock, stress, PTSD, *something* is going on in my brain because water doesn't just rise up and attack people. I'm seeing things.

Emma's forehead wrinkles, and she puts a hand on my knee and squeezes. "I know we haven't had much chance to talk, but if you need—"

I swallow again, forcing saliva around a lump in my throat. "It's fine. I'm okay." I'm not. My heart jolts and jangles in my chest like I've clamped my hands around an electric fence, but what else am I supposed to say? "I'm sorry for shouting earlier."

She sighs. "You just lost your best friend, I'll give you some slack."

I nod and get out of the car. The shack is dim inside, the curtains are drawn and there's dirty dishes in the sink from two days ago. I couldn't bring myself to eat last night. Emma guides me to the couch, and I don't resist. The place still smells like Mitch. Sweat and salt.

For a while Emma sits with me, watching in silence, trying to figure out what's going through my head. Not for the first time I feel inadequate under her gaze. She's too good for me, really. We've been dating since high school, but where all I've done is get a job at a fish and chip shop and spend my weekends surfing and getting drunk, she's preparing to do honours in marine biology. Every day she grows more distant, like a ship sailing for the horizon, leaving me behind on the shore; our worlds irrevocably sundered.

After ten minutes she gets up and goes to the kitchen. There's a clink of heavy bottles, followed by two distinct pops, and she walks back into the lounge with a beer in each hand. She passes me one.

"Thanks." The word feels thick in my mouth.

"To Mitch," she says.

We clink the bottles together and drink. The beer is cold and fizzes down my throat. Frothy, like the sea. The thought nearly makes me choke.

When she finishes her beer, Emma rises from the couch, her shape silhouetted against the TV I'm pretending to watch so I don't have to talk. "You hungry?"

I shrug. I'm not, but I should probably eat something.

"I'll call some takeout, yeah?"

I nod, and belatedly dig into my pocket for my wallet. She's already in the kitchen placing the order—pizza it sounds like—so I put it down on the coffee table for when the food comes. I sink back into the couch, staring at the paint-flaking ceiling, wondering what I'm supposed to tell her.

Hey babe, so it seems the sea has it in for me. Well, not just the sea, any form of water really.

Put it like that and it sounds even more ridiculous. She won't believe me. Hell, I'm not even sure I do. Emma's the least superstitious person I know, the kind of person who rolls her eyes in horror movies at the sheer impracticality of the plot. She and Mitch never got along, not unless I was there to bridge the gap. I'm mulling over it again when I make out a distinct slosh and clank from the kitchen. I sigh. Emma is doing the dishes.

Just bloody leave them.

And my thoughts falter. She's doing the dishes. With *water.*

I lurch to my feet. Five strides and I'm in the kitchen. Emma's back is to me, up to her elbows in it, rubber-clad gloves scrubbing at a pot.

"Emma, no!"

It probably happens in a moment. A few heartbeats at most. But time slows down for me. In the sink, the water ripples and gathers. Emma's arm jerks still, as if someone, *something* has grabbed it.

There's an intake of breath. A short sharp hush through her teeth. She stiffens; all the muscles in her shoulders tense.

"What the fu—"

The water in the sink rises; a tendril emerging from the murk. It latches around Emma's arm.

She screams.

The water surges up her arms, the grimy suds pumping upward. They soak into her shirt, writhing towards her throat.

No, please no. Not Emma.

I lunge, grab her and yank her back, breaking the tendril's hold, splattering water over the floor. Emma's already thrashing. Her fingers claw at her face—at her mouth and nose—and the water keeps on coming. It condenses over her cheeks, forcing itself through her lips and up her nose. She's coughing, spluttering, eyes wide, pupils dark pinpricks before they roll back into her head.

It's in her. Whatever it is, it's in her. Drowning her.

I do the only thing I can think of. I punch her in the chest. Hard. Something pops in my fist and pain blossoms across my knuckles. Emma convulses. Water bubbles from her lips, then slips back down.

Idiot, she needs to be on her side. Recovery position, remember? A memory of a swim-safe class rises inside me. Dr ABCD. A is for airways. Clear the airways.

Cold sweat rolls off me as I turn her over and slam a hand between her shoulder blades. "Get out!" I scream and strike again. "Get out!" This last one sounds more like a plea. I open her mouth, strike a third time.

Her body jerks, coughs, and water slops out of her and onto the floor. I pull the tea towel down from the drainage board and dump it over the pool. The towel soaks it in. I hope it's enough.

B is for breathing.

And she's not breathing. I roll her onto her back, hands shaking. "Come on." I pinch her nose, put my mouth to hers and puff. Yes! Her chest rises one, two, three times. I do it twice more. Emma vomits up more water, more than I thought possible, and then, a glorious sound: a single ragged breath.

I push her onto her side again—more coughing—and she takes another breath, stronger this time, then another. She doesn't wake. But she's alive. Alive. I slump against the fridge, wipe away the sweat and tears, and dig out my phone.

And for the second time in two days, I dial triple zero.

"You saved her life," the paramedic says as Emma is wheeled away on a stretcher.

Slipped in the bathroom, knocked herself out on the lip of the bath and fell into it. That's the story I told. It was the best I could come up with. Horgan scowls as I recount it to him, standing there in the driveway, the blue lights of his car still flashing across the weatherboards. He doesn't believe me. But there's no evidence of foul play. No one to discredit my story. Not Mitch. Not Emma—not until she's conscious anyway, and her story will make even less sense than mine. Horgan's got nothing and he knows it.

"Don't leave town," he tells me as a paramedic asks him to move his car to let the ambulance out of the driveway.

"You can follow behind us," the paramedic says, sliding in behind the wheel of the van. Meat wagons—that's what Emma liked to call them. I used to laugh at that, but now, thinking of Emma's cold, shivering body inside, it sounds sick.

You sick fucks. The comment from the video swims up from my memory. We should never have posted it. Shouldn't even have done it. That's when it all started.

"You good to drive?" The paramedic asks. "Hospital's not far."

I shake my head. I can't risk it. Won't. "I need to call her Mum. Let her know what's happened."

The paramedic shrugs. "As you please."

As they pull out from the driveway, I take out Emma's phone and stare at the message again. I found it on the kitchen counter, unlocked, as if she'd been waiting to read it.

BFF Kirsty
I know it's bad timing, but you need to end it. Don't drag it out.

I should cry, scream maybe. Instead, I'm hollow. Spent. I walk back inside and call Emma's Mum.

The knock comes on the door three days later. I shuffle past takeaway containers and empty juice bottles to open it, cracking the door a finger-width and peering out. Two suits stand on the doorstep: one man, one woman. He's broad shouldered and bald. She's shorter, brown hair cut into a bob so straight I could hold a ruler to it.

"Mr." The woman consults her notebook. "Holloway?"

I shift behind the door, conscious of the smell that must be emanating through the crack. I ran out of deodorant yesterday. But the suits are waiting, so I work enough spittle to wet my throat.

"Yea?" I rasp.

"We'd like to ask you a few questions about the video you posted."

The video? I stare at them, taking in their sharp suits and immaculate shoes. Detectives from the city perhaps? Though I see nothing that looks like a badge.

"It was a hoax," I say. "A fake. A prank to try and make money. The animals were already dead, I swear." *It was Mitch's idea,* I want to say, but instead I bite down on the words. swallow, eyes turning hot, despite not having enough water left in me for tears. My head is pounding.

The woman gives me a closed lipped smile—almost a grimace. "Oh, we know. We're more interested in what's happened *since* you posted it."

Her partner produces bottled water from behind his back and holds it out. It takes everything I have not to flinch. *It's in a bottle. It's contained.*

"You must be thirsty," the woman says.

I lock my knees to hide their wobble and hold onto the door handle as my stomach does a complete 360. My face must be a picture.

"It's safe," the woman assures me. Her partner waves the bottle, and I'm transfixed, quivering like a rat before a snake. "May we come in?"

They know. How do they know? And they *believe* it. Believe me. *But I haven't told anyone.* Except for Horgan, but I don't think he even deemed my statement worth noting down. *Perhaps they have answers.* I waver a second longer, then open the door. *Maybe they have a solution.* Hope flickers inside me at that.

I lead them through the rental to the lounge and they pull up two chairs while I take the couch. I perch on its edge, conscious of the house's smell—and mine. I've done my best since I turned off the water mains, ordering takeout (burning a hole in my bank account in the process), peeing on the lemon tree out back, shitting in a pit I dug by the shed. I'm managing.

Sort of. But the moment it rains, I'm dead.

The man presents the water bottle. I hesitate for a heartbeat, then grab it, crack the lid and put it to my lips. Cool, sweet water trickles into my mouth, and suddenly I'm gulping, sucking it down in great mouthfuls. God it's good. I force myself to slow down, enjoy it. Sip. My headache eases.

I wipe my mouth with my sleeve. "How did you know? About the water, I mean. Have you seen it be—"

"It's our job to watch Father's enemies," the woman says.

I falter, not sure I heard right. "Come again?"

"You've offended him. Dues must be paid," the man shifts forward in his chair. It's the first time he's spoken, and his voice is deep, a baritone that shivers in my chest. The woman puts a hand on his knee.

"Easy Kaito."

Kaito's enormous hands twitch on his lap, but otherwise he doesn't move. I swallow, taking in his barrel chest and bulging arms, and shift in my seat. I don't fancy my chances if he decides to take a swing at me.

"What did you say your names were?"

"We didn't," the woman says. She places a hand on her chest. "I am Mira and he is Kaito." She indicates her colleague. "We are envoys." She pulls down her collar, and there, where her collarbone meets her neck are three dark, parallel marks. Tattoos. Each one the length of my little finger and ridged like a fresh scar. I glance at Kaito; a set of three marks pokes out the top of his collar. Are they from a gang? A chill shivers over my skin and I lurch to my feet.

"Look, I don't want any trouble."

"Trouble?" Mira's eyes flash. "You're long past trouble. Now *sit.*"

The muscles in my legs spasm. My knees buckle. I sway, fighting to stay on my feet. Mira's gaze locks with mine, her head tilts and a vein pulses in her temple. Then my knees curl, bend against my will, sinking me down, *sitting* me back on the couch.

What the fu—

Mira leans forward and grins. My stomach turns: her teeth are filed into points.

"Did you know up to 60 per cent of the human body is water? It's everywhere, even in your bones."

I freeze, horror yawning inside me, deep and cold and absolute. Yes, I have heard that before. Sometime long ago in school, probably biology class. The water in my stomach churns again and I almost feel it flushing out into my veins.

I open my mouth, start to speak, but Mira raises a finger and my jaw locks. "Hush, hush. It is easier on all of us if you go quietly." She turns to Kaito. "Did you bring it?"

The bald man nods and draws out a knife two fingers wide and as long as my palm. It is rusted and old, as if it's spent the last ten years on the sea bed. Perhaps it has.

"What are you—" I manage to get out before Mira's finger jerks up again, and the water in my stomach rises. Acid burns the back of my throat. Then water washes into my mouth and it's . . . salty. Like the sea. I try to scream, but it comes out a gurgle of bubbles and brine. *This can't be happening. This can't be real.* But it is. The water plunges down my throat, into my lungs, flooding them in cold.

They're drowning you.

My body jerks and twitches and I slide to the floor. My skin itches. The water inside me churns, gurgles in my throat. I'm paralysed. Unable to move, not even blink.

"Father does not forgive," Kaito rumbles.

They were already dead, I want to scream at them. *We only wanted a bit of extra cash for summer.* And are they growing larger? Or am I growing smaller?

"Father does not forget," Mira echoes. I can't feel my legs. Or my hands. White hairs swirl in my peripheral—they're coming from my face. I'm screaming at my limbs. *Move, please, just move!* My lungs burn, desperate for air.

Kaito presses the knife to my neck. *This is it, he's going to—*

With three deft strokes, he scores the parallel scratches above my collarbone. Then again on the other side. My body jerks and convulses. My vision shifts. Something wet slaps the floorboards, and I catch a sliver of orange and pink in the evening light.

"You are at the ocean's mercy now."

At once, the water's grip vanishes. I flop and stare up at them, gasping, groping for air. No not air, *water*. It's already in my lungs. I breathe it in, feel the cool rush up my airways and out the gills Kaito's scored on my neck.

"Better get you back to the sea, pup," says Mira. "Best not keep Father waiting."

The two of them grin, their honed teeth flashing.

And all I can do is bleat.

About the Author:

Nikky grew up as a barefoot 90s child in Perth, Western Australia, before moving to New Zealand in 2016. By day she works as a professional content writer and by night authors speculative fiction, often burning the candle at both ends to explore fantastic worlds, mine asteroids and meet wizards. Her creative work has appeared in magazines, on radio and in anthologies around the world. She is currently writing a dark fantasy trilogy, routinely sacrificing literary darlings to the editing gods in the hopes of seeing it published.

You can find her online at
W:nikkythewriter.com | T:@NikkyMLee | F:nikkythewriter

LORD OF THE DEEP

Marcus Turner

The deep trembles. So it begins anew, rippling the still waters of both thought and space with its idiot mewling—a newborn screaming its way into existence.

Endless hunger, the bawling darkness that precedes all things.

Chaos born yet again.

The deep trembles, and the hoary eyes crack open, crusty with the sleep of ages. Hunger, and hate, growl awake. Entwined lovers shiver in trepidation and lunatic lust; infants start screaming—nameless terror vexing soul and sinew. Fathers grind their teeth in unplaceable rage and despair, calamity shivering in their bones. Mothers hold their bellies, a graveyard rotting foreshadowed in their wombs.

The waters ripple, quivering like stricken flesh. A new age, a break in the eternal conflict, is imminent. Such darkness— something has shifted.

So it begins anew . . . to end at long last.

The creature was back, watching him as he slept for the fourth night in a row.

It looked like a man at first, ripped out of time. A thick, plaited black beard, dark kohl-rimmed eyes. Bare-chested and bronzed, he stood wearing only a long, rough-spun skirt, and a horned helmet shaped like a sharply ridged turtle shell. Its presence in the shadowy corner pricked Magnus awake through the blanket of sleep. The stranger stood smiling, lips pallid and bloodless in the small spot of moonlight illuminating its face, making silvery flares of his eyes.

What made Magnus' blood freeze wasn't the uncanny fact of a strange voyeur invading the privacy of sleep, but the instinctive awareness that it wasn't a man at all. It was a rind, a skin to be peeled back from some rotting fruit.

At last, the entity didn't seem to care any longer to pretend. The giveaway was the horns. Gone were the horns and helmet of previous nights; tonight, *real* horns emerged from the figure's forehead, thick and long, curving back like a ram's. And then there was the auburn-coloured fur sprouting from what had previously been smooth skin—threading through pores before Magnus' eyes, like watching a time-lapse video, until eventually no skin could be seen at all.

The face was changing, too. The nose and mouth were drawing closer together while the face elongated. The eyes changed from brown to a harrowing ice-blue, while the pupils contorted into horizontal slits. The creature's lips turned black, became leathery and animalistic—but that leering smile did not change.

It lapped up his fear like milk, and it was *thirsty*.

The devil, he thought. *I'm being haunted by the devil.*

The skirt became leather; the bones beneath fused together, a grotesque syndactylous digit, before the flesh took on an oily shimmer. Scales—a thick tail tapering into a broad fan of pearlescent black fins.

He had seen photos of the Horned Goat, Baphomet, Satan . . . but this wasn't any of those beasts. This was the Goat of Waters, the Living Capricorn. Lord of the Deep.

How the hell did I know that?

A shiver prickled Magnus' arms.

"Who are you?" Magnus demanded.

The creature's smile split open, but instead of worn, square goat's teeth, its mouth was filled with daggers. It flensed the air with them, stretching and testing its jaws, before it finally rasped a single guttural word:

"*Apsuuuu.*"

"What?" Magnus cried, revolted by the horrible voice.

"*Apsu.*" The Goat of Waters lifted its clawed arms to the ceiling. A rush of waters—a sloshing of waves breaking against walls and bedposts.

Black water disgorged from the carpet, flooding the room at alarming speed. Water seeped through the mattress, spilling over its edges. Magnus cried out, but the moment the water touched him, his body refused to obey his screaming mind. He was anchored to the bed by some invisible force while the water engulfed him, pouring down his throat. It rose past the window, obscuring the moonlight. The inky form of the Lord of the Deep continued to watch Magnus as he drowned.

The Apsu, *the Apsu . . .*

Magnus woke like a man rising from the bottom of a lake, coughing and spluttering. The sun coming in through his window couldn't cut through the chill permeating his skin. But it had been no dream—he knew that as well as he knew the lines on his hand, the moles on his face and neck. He could still feel the icy water pouring down his throat, the sodden sponges of his lungs . . . He'd drowned. He'd *died.* And yet here he was.

How strange that a dead man could feel so fresh and energised, so *alive*; born anew from the baptismal waters of terror and pandemonium.

Magnus got out of bed and headed to the bathroom, wondering why his relatively dry sheets were at such odds with his memory. *The room flooded. I drowned. It wasn't a fucking dream.*

I'm not crazy.

The person looking back at him in the mirror looked surprisingly fresh for a man drowned by a murderous, evil presence. But then dreaming of drowning probably hurt a lot worse than *actual* drowning, because the brief terror overloaded the senses, made what was merely common and pedestrian somehow special, meaningful. But there was nothing special or exceptional about death, the brief, clawing struggle.

But you know it wasn't a dream. Something happened. Something has changed. You know it, don't you?

And then, the burning question: *What is the Apsu?*

The Apsu. The mere thought of the word covered his skin with gooseflesh, and a formless dread twisted in slimy coils in his guts.

It had awoken. It was hungry—and he was the prey. The Goat of Waters smiled again in his memory, flashing its rows of long, needle-like teeth. *Why me?*

Surely a god did not register a man, the slimy afterbirth of the universe's womb. *Unless you're not a man. Not anymore.*

Magnus backed away from his reflection. *Maybe you are losing your marbles, son.*

He went downstairs into the kitchen. His sister Leila was already at the table, scrolling through her phone as she nursed a cup of coffee in her free hand. Magnus went to the cupboard, took out a bowl and joined her at the table, reaching for the box of Corn Flakes.

"You're up late," Leila said, without looking up.

Magnus stood back up and went to get the milk and a spoon, then returned to the table without replying.

"You missed the bus, *and* the train. You're going to be late for work. Again. It's—"

"9:37 a.m. I know." He glanced at his naked wrist. He'd left both his smart-watch and his phone upstairs, but somehow, *he knew.* He knew the exact second of where they stood in time.

Leila looked at him with a lopsided frown. "Yeeeah. Anyway, you're late. You're probably gonna get fired. This is, what, the sixth or seventh time in a month?"

"I'm not going in today," Magnus answered through a mouthful of milk and half-chewed cereal.

Leila threw up her hands in exasperation. "Even better."

Magnus continued shovelling food into his mouth without rebuttal. Leila stood up—she was already dressed for work in her black pencil skirt and collared shirt. The diamond pendant on her white-gold necklace gleamed in the morning light. "Anyway, some of us have to get to work."

Magnus grunted. It was his go-to communication with his sister—he knew she hated it, though he never intended to bait her. But the shark was ever circling, and as always, she lunged.

"Do you even care?" Leila blurted.

"About what?"

"About *anything?* Fucking hell, you live your life in a daze. Zero consideration for the impact your actions have on anyone else." She wrung her hair in her hands. "I'm not your mum, Magnus."

"I know that," he replied peevishly.

"Well, when are you going to start acting like you realise that? I'm not her replacement and I don't fucking want to be.

We're supposed to be in this together, helping each other get by until we're in a position to go our separate ways. But you act as if it's an option. It's not."

"What do you want me to say?" *That I don't care, because as of 2:44pm today, both our worlds are about to change.*

Whoa, where did that come from?

"That you'll call work, *apologise profusely* for being late yet *again*, and beg them not to fire your ass—if not for your own sake, then your sister's," said Leila.

It won't matter. I won't need food or shelter after today. Neither will you, because you'll be dead.

"Are you going to say anything at all?" she demanded.

"Like what?"

"'Sorry' might be a good start."

Magnus turned his head and rolled his eyes, so she wouldn't see; but she probably knew anyway. If she hadn't sensed his absolute indifference at this twilight hour of her life, she never would. "Well, sorry, then."

Leila scoffed, unimpressed. "It's only our lives, for God's sake."

At 2:44pm, it'll only be my life. And in the blink of an eye, the future unspooled before his eyes, a ribbon ripped by tragedy. *An accident. A car is going to crash through the window of Michael Hill's. It's not a hit-and-run robbery as the media will speculate, just a stupid accident. The tank is going to catch on fire. That whole corner of the Westfield is going to burn. The driver, and all the Michael Hill employees are going to die, including Leila.*

Leila screwed up her face. "You're being even weirder than usual."

"Don't go to work today," Magnus said.

"What? Why?"

"Just a . . . bad feeling, that's all."

Leila grinned, hand on her hip. "Right. So I'm supposed to risk losing my job for your *feeling?*"

Magnus shrugged and turned back to his cereal.

"No, really. What's going on?" she asked.

You won't listen. You never do, and you look for any excuse to get away from me, because secretly I've always made you uncomfortable. You asked Mum about it once, and she said you were being silly, that I cared and felt things, I just didn't show it. You weren't convinced—still aren't. Magnus' mind overflowed with secret knowledge, past and future gleanings. *I could tell you, but you won't believe me, and you'll go to work to die anyway.*

My God, what is going on with me? Where is all this shit coming from?

"Nothing. Sorry," Magnus said. "Have a nice day at work."

It was hard to feel guilty, no matter how hard he tried to force the feeling, to forcibly will it to galvanise him into action before it was too late. But it was no use, he realised as he stared at the blank TV: you couldn't change what was already future-past.

God damn it, where was all this *coming from?*

He lit up his phone screen and checked the time: 1:32pm. He set an alarm and put the phone back down on the armrest.

2:44 came and went. Magnus didn't turn the TV on straight away, knowing it wouldn't make the news for a little while yet.

At 2:55pm he turned on the TV. A newsflash was just beginning.

"Breaking news now from Westfield Airport West in Melbourne's north-west," the blonde anchor-woman said, staring solemnly down the camera, "a car has reportedly crashed through the wall of the shopping centre and ploughed into the Michael Hill Jewellers, before exploding moments later. Witnesses allege the car lost control and veered off the road. It does not appear at this time to have been a deliberate 'ram-raid'. We have no further information on casualties right now, stay tuned for more as this story develops."

The Goat of Waters watched from beside the entertainment unit, smiling.

"You motherfucker," Magnus growled, though he knew the Goat had nothing to do with it—blaming the creature simply made him feel better. He'd tried to convince himself of his own guilt, too, but he didn't believe that either, even if others might see fit to blame him. But they didn't see what he saw. They didn't *know*.

He knew this because knowledge was the gift of his awakening. The workings of the universe's machinery, the weave and weft of fate, the mysteries of creation—secret and forbidden things he had no earthly way of knowing. It was through this he understood that fate was as solid as stone—it could be broken, worn down with enough time and energy expended, but it would always reform; fate, once written, would come about, one way or the other. Understanding bloomed like a kaleidoscopic rainbow bursting outwards at light speed, fractals exploding upon fractals with every heartbeat—yet understanding did not make the truth any less galling.

He was becoming a *god*.

How is that even possible? Not because the idea was impossible—many had come before him—but at the same time, there were no gods . . . None *living*, anyway. None but the Apsu, the Primordial Remnant, the Goat of Waters, Lord of the Deep. *Until now.*

Magnus' mind recoiled, warring against the forces of creation and destruction oscillating in his fevered mind like converging galaxies, a cosmic collision of his humanity and nascent godhood—and a few lingering splinters of confusion and self-doubt for good measure—vomiting out of his egg-shell skull.

He sat and mourned his sister in the only way his soul permitted: a complex equation not fully grasped.

Magnus sat on his bed, his hands circling around an orb of light like a miniature sun. Slowly, he flattened his palms and spread his hands apart, stretching the light along with it. This was the stuff of creation: the mesh beneath physicality; the invisible force binding all matter made incandescent and malleable like molten iron.

His phone screen lit up and vibrated for the twentieth time. He did not answer—the call would contain nothing meaningful to him.

His right hand glided along the bottom edge of the bar of light, began to hone it into a sword's edge with his fingertips—a smith playing in the forge of the gods.

Why was this happening—to *him*? How was it even possible? Although knowledge continued to explode within him, each detonation igniting the next, like an AI hurtling towards singularity, the answers to those questions still eluded him. It was as if some *other*, some power beyond reckoning, deliberately obfuscated him, a bulging black abscess in his mind. Something didn't want him to know. But still, *why?* Why him? He was not special.

Maybe your mind is perfectly suited for what's happening to you. Wisdom and perception unmarred by sentimentality.

The Goat of Waters came and went, flickering in and out of reality to watch him. *An avatar, not the real beast.* Magnus ignored it as best he could, though he felt ill at ease practising his new powers with it watching. It was sizing him up. But Magnus was feeling less disturbed by its presence as he grew more confident in his experimentations. Could its increasing presence, its boldness, be nothing more than posturing? A mask for its fear?

No, he decided, as he met the Goat's gaze, evaluating its smirk. *Not fear—excitement. It calls to me. It wants me to come.*

Apsu, Apsu, the Goat hissed in confirmation as the twilight filled his bedroom with ominous shadows.

The Apsu—the one thing he needed to know, to understand; yet it was the one thing hidden from his newborn eyes. *A blockage.*

Magnus went to his desk, sat down and opened his laptop. He typed *Apsu* into the search bar and scanned the results page. An acronym for some type of business—nothing useful there. Above the search bar, Google asked, *Did you mean "abzu"?* Magnus clicked the link. *Abzu* and *Apsu*—used interchangeably in Sumerian, Akkadian, Babylonian mythology: the primeval sea in the bowels of the world, the void space between the earth and the underworld.

Magnus frowned. Aquifers? Underground seas between the earth and underworld? It still didn't explain why the Goat kept haunting him, nor the monumental powers transforming him.

Wait . . . What if the Apsu is the place where it lives, the primeval sea? Is it trying to make me go there, to meet it face to face?

A scan through Wikipedia and then a website on Mesopotamian mythology brought more information: the Apsu wasn't just a place, but an entity existing within it—a primordial chaos god. Several references caught his eye: *Apsu*, the Begetter. The Dreamer.

The Devourer.

My father. The thought screamed through his limbs, searing nerves like arcing electricity.

It didn't make sense. If the Apsu—the Goat—was the Begetter, the Father, then . . . where were all the other gods?

The names are not mutually exclusive, but parts of a process: there are no gods because the Apsu births them and then devours them. It devours its children because it is afraid of them.

Magnus turned his head. The Goat of Waters loomed again beside his bed, smiling. He ignored it and continued reading.

The Apsu feared its children, feared their rising power, and so it devoured them, to maintain its dominion. And yet in its slumber it continued to spawn new gods beyond its control, born from its dreams and nightmares. It woke only when its newborn progeny let out their birthing wail . . . to murder them, to *eat . . .*

An icy knife cut all the way down along his spine. So even gods could know fear.

Magnus rose and approached the Goat, mere inches away from its undulating fangs. The creature's smile yawned wider. Only a projection, an extension of the real demon, but it could speak . . . and it could listen.

"Tell me where to go," he demanded, jaw clenching. "Tell me how to find the Apsu."

The Living Capricorn reached up with a clawed finger and pushed it through Magnus' brow as if skin and bone were soft butter. Magnus cried out softly in alarm, before the finger anchored itself in his cortex.

To pursue the Apsu is to march willingly to the grave, the Goat whispered—a complexity and humanness of thought that its crude mouth could never have imitated. *So many have come before you—Enki, Zeus, Horus, Loki, Quetzalcoatl, even the Judeo-Christian upstart—all have fallen to the Apsu. So is its decree—all gods must die. None are suffered to live but the*

Apsu; none escape the Devourer's gaze. And yet you would offer yourself up, a babe begging the slaughterer's knife?

You are but a squalling newborn. What power do you have to battle the Apsu? What inkling *have you of the madness?*

Magnus could not find words to answer. A litany of the dead, the names of extinguished gods from every human pantheon—even names of gods in a thousand alien tongues from places beyond the visible stars—babbled through his mind like a river of ghosts. And the implications! A godless world, a godless *universe,* except for the Apsu: a predatory, megalomaniac force of chaos and darkness. *A prophecy.*

A prophecy he unwittingly accelerated with idiotic bravery.

"Tell me," Magnus insisted against the creeping despair frosting his insides. "Tell me where to find the Apsu. Where to find *you.*"

The Goat flashed its unholy rings of teeth—whether in delight or mockery, Magnus couldn't tell; perhaps they were one and the same. Images flooded through the Goat's invading finger into Magnus' mind: a peninsula; a massive freshwater lake. A place he recognised from family holidays with Leila and his mother.

River grass waving gently in the murky depths.

He knew where he had to go, what he had to do.

Magnus didn't call work or stay to organise his sister's funeral. Such things seemed irrelevant, so small, in the light of what lay ahead. For all the immense power that coursed through his limbs, all the preternatural intelligence now setting his every neuron aglow, nothing could alleviate the sense of doom crushing down on him like the full weight of the ocean.

Human concerns simply *did not matter.*

After a three-and-a-half-hour road-trip out of Melbourne,

the massive body of water, and the knobby finger of land extending across it, soared into view: Lake Eildon.

Magnus turned off the highway away from Eildon and continued down towards Jerusalem Creek. He parked the car inside the holiday park and strolled through to the lake's edge. The park was only half-full, being outside the holiday season—mostly caravaners stopping over for the night, and a few permanent residents. Except for a lone fishing boat far out beyond Gerraty Bay, the lake was lonely and still; ominous, as if all souls sensed the cataclysmic echo of what was to come, and though unable to explain their misgivings, stayed away.

He made sure no-one was out walking by the lake before stepping into the water, not bothering to take off his clothes or shoes. He waded out past the shallows, then broke into a freestyle swim towards the deeper, darker cobalt waters. The water soon swelled as a monstrous black mouth beneath him— he'd come far enough.

Magnus stretched out on his back, floating for a moment before bowing his torso and allowing himself to sink. The Goat of Waters slipped into view from the darkness below, swam over and placed a hairy claw on his chest, pressing him down. A moment passed between them, a kind of candour: whatever happened today would change the world forever.

His lungs suddenly cramped. Magnus forced more air from his lungs, but his body refused the dreadful demand heaped upon it. *Relent,* he whispered . . . But the crazed animal inside him struggled, frothing in desperate fury.

Magnus sank faster. The Lord of the Deep smiled. The shell yielded at last, expelling the last motes of air inside its lungs. A second baptism before a passage opened into unfathomable darkness. Into death.

Magnus thrust himself upwards, exploding across the surface of the subterranean lake like a great white shark, thrashing with alarm. Another death, another baptismal drowning—and yet he could breathe. No coughing, no water flooding his lungs. Strange.

It was so dark that it was impossible to tell where the water ended and the cavern began. It took several moments for Magnus' eyes to adjust, to separate the water and the void to discern his surroundings. Thin grey stalactites dangled above like wheeling chandeliers of knives. The cave walls curved round and extended into the distance like the gullet of a monstrous serpent. A little further into the cavern, an even darker shadow rose up out of the lapping waters—some kind of edifice. Trudging closer, through the waist-deep water, squinting against the gloom, he saw it was a squat stone temple, encrusted with calcium and other mineral growths. No braziers glowed inside its gates; no hymns resonated from its hidden cloisters. A forgotten, forsaken place.

What men would have—*could* have—built a temple in such a place?

Unless the builders were not men at all?

Magnus knew the answer as soon as the thought crossed his mind. *The first gods. They built this.*

But if they honoured the Apsu . . . why did it destroy them? Why does it continue to murder us?

Something rose from the shallows he'd just departed—something far too big to be concealed even in such depths. A famished rumbling; the saurian crackle of a disused throat; a hot, rank exhalation like wind through a bushfire.

Suddenly the braziers along the temple's staircase erupted to life: it was not fire, but living *water* that took the shape of flames, flickering, scintillating with bioluminescent light. It did not glow as brightly as flame and threw the temple and the nearby rock formations into greater relief—and everything else into greater shadow.

Slowly, Magnus turned. A barely perceptible form slithered and shifted its massive bulk in the darkness; a miasma of death and rotting, eons-old god-flesh wafting on its breath.

The Apsu.

Its ancient and reptilian voice ground like tectonic plates inside Magnus' skull. *Newborn. What do you call yourself?*

"Magnus."

A deep, rumbling growl. *Not your before-name.*

"This is my only one." All the power inside him became like water, threatening to flow down his legs. Whatever strength he had, here in this demon's presence, it counted for nothing.

What were gods compared to *this?*

It matters not. Curious as this one may be, it will not change the cycle: you will die, as all gods must. I will eat, and then sleep peacefully for millennia to come. It is the natural order.

"I didn't want to be a god. I *don't.*"

Desire is irrelevant. You are a god. That is all that matters.

"Why must the gods die?"

Another disdainful growl. *Why do you ask such questions? Knowing is your Aspect: this I know as well as you.*

"I can't see everything."

You lie.

"You fear competition."

The Apsu's six black eyes, like teardrops of polished obsidian, bolted open. Magnus sensed a sneer on its scaly lips.

You scratch at the surface of things possessing depths you cannot fathom. I am older than time, boy: I have watched, for endless ages, the turmoil the gods would wreak upon the universe; seen the greed and lust girding their loins to rape the world and its people.

This one made a choice: to deliver the cosmos, they must

be empty. *The evil children must die.*

"Is it not the role of fathers to guide their sons and daughters, to discipline and tutor them? Don't children emulate the natures of their parents?"

The Apsu hissed in disgust. *You know nothing, infant. The first children proved only the error of such notions as control. They could not be contained. Tiamat and I, our union—one of love—it created monsters! It begat fickle, wicked creatures that would bring* order *only to serve their own ends, to enslave softer, more gullible beings. At first they honoured us, but it was a deception: the children declared war against us, led by Enki. Enki killed Tiamat, cut her body into a hundred pieces and mortally wounded this one with his blasphemous weapons.*

I brought a thousand hells' worth of wrath crashing down upon them. Death, and oblivion.

How I mourned! Tiamat, ripped to pieces by the fruit of her own womb! In despair, I consumed her pieces, so that my consort might live on forever inside my belly, be one with me always. That was my mistake: the children should have ended with Tiamat's avenging. Instead the mother's fertility took root in this one's slumbering mind—the Apsu bore more children, more wicked gods to plague the cosmos, through its dreams.

So began this one's purpose: a bulwark to guard against the savage gods; the preservation of a peaceful, unsullied universe.

"But the world *isn't* peaceful, Apsu. Humans kill each other, wage war, steal, rape. Their cruelty knows no bounds. What does your murder achieve, then?"

The universe does not need gods to magnify what mortals do perfectly well on their own. Your argument yet justifies my end.

"Gods might instruct them—lead them away from their darkness, if given the chance—"

Enough! I weary of this prattle.

"So that's it?" Magnus snarled, shaking his head. "I'm sentenced to die because I was selected by the universe's cosmic lottery? It's not fair."

I must prevent the pestilence, as only I can. I am the Primordial Vestige—the last remnant of Chaos. The only one strong enough to end the madness . . .

"The Goat of Waters, The Living Capricorn, Lord of the Deep—all your stupid names. I don't care what you are. *You* are the evil one. *You* are the monster."

The hidden serpentine head turned on its side; the black eyes, glossier than the surrounding darkness, narrowed to suspicious slits, scrutinising him for a long time.

Then, the voice, limned with something unfamiliar: doubt.

You don't know who you are, do you?

"What?"

The Goat stood watching him from the Apsu's left flank. The bearded man with the four-tiered crown—its earlier manifestation—stood on the Apsu's right, holding a spear. Both beamed tight-lipped, sinister smiles—as if privy to some terrible secret.

I am not the Goat of Waters. That was Enki's first form. It is **you**, *newborn. Enki, my first spawn, reborn.*

"What?" Magnus' eyes widened. How had his *gift* not made any of this known?

The Apsu shifted closer. The first clear impression of a horned black-scaled dragon head twisting lifted from the shadows like crags rising from the primordial soup. Innumerable fangs glistened in the soft bioluminescence cast by the temple's braziers. The Apsu's growl sounded almost like a long, throaty cackle.

I shall enjoy devouring you once more, my murderous son. Eating you a thousand times over is not enough to avenge all you have done . . .

The Apsu charged forward, open maw dripping. The cavern shook; stalactites broke from the ceiling and sent geysers exploding from the waters. The stench of dead gods flooded the cave.

Magnus smiled.

A spark of light as the Apsu loomed over him—a radiant bar that vanished impossibly fast but for a tiny remaining splinter in the burgeoning black.

The Apsu let out a cavern-shaking roar. Oily black blood boiled from its mouth into the water.

The abscess, the black fruit of ignorance, was suddenly gone.

The Apsu wailed and stamped its feet but could not move. The haft of the spear of light jutted from its back, pinning it to the floor. Magnus grinned. It had suspected—now it *knew*.

If only it hadn't been blindsided by that flicker of doubt.

"You should have swallowed me when you had the chance."

Deceiver! the Apsu screeched in outrage. *How? How!*

"Knowledge is my Aspect, Father. It helps me see a great deal . . . perhaps too much. You would never have believed my ignorance . . . unless I really *was* ignorant. You have lived too long to be fooled so easily. But if I could fool even myself, then I could fool *you*." His smile broadened in triumph.

"From the moment I drew breath, before you'd even rubbed the grit of sleep from your eyes, I placed a block in the shell's mind, so it could not know who and what I was, or what you were. Only impressions could be permitted. A gambit—so much depending on but a moment of apprehension, a sliver of weakness . . ."

You truly are Enki, little deceiver.

"No," Magnus replied, the mirth sliding from his face like melted wax. "Enki is dead. But all newborns are echoes of those that have come before. Sekhmet, Ares, Huītzilōpōchtli, Týr—all shades of the only true-born god of war, Irra. Thoth, Apollo, Odin, Fukurokuju—spectres of Enki! Ghosts of the past born into reality by your frightful dreams.

"But this time, you had a particularly bad dream. In it you saw Enki and Irra—relived your wife's murder at Enki's hand all over again; witnessed once more the devastation Irra wreaked upon ancient Babylon—and then you imagined something *inconceivable*:

"What if Enki and Irra were *one*?"

The Apsu roared, spraying black spittle. It squirmed upon the impaling spear, thrusting up on its thick legs, trying to unpin itself. With a sliding of the hands and a simple thought, another incandescent spear appeared in Magnus' hands and he drove it through the Apsu's flank, piercing all the way through its ribcage. The monster screamed and dropped to the floor, shivering. *No . . .*

"I have no name, Father—but I will give myself one fit to honour the delirious horror of your nightmares." His voice boomed: *"I am Enkirra—Scourge of Chaos, Avenger of the Gods; the All-Knowing, All-Seeing Avatar of War and Plagues, The Goat of Waters, The Living Capricorn . . . "*

Magnus was gone. Enkirra swelled within its host shell, luminous like a thousand suns. He smiled, and his shell's mouth bristled with rings of the Goat's needle fangs. "The *new* Lord of the Deep."

The Apsu struggled but the fight was draining from it, oily ichor pouring from its wounds. The obsidian eyes were losing their sheen. Enkirra conjured a third spear and calmly approached the Apsu.

The world deserves better than you, the Apsu groaned. *You will bring nothing but destruction and despair!*

"No. They will fight each other to win my favour, but in

45

their worship, their savage devotion, there will be unity. Through love and fear I will bind a hundred warring nations, a thousand errant faiths. I will be the only god: the god of everything.

"And *you,* Apsu, will be nothing but a brief memory. A forgotten myth on a dusty, broken tablet."

Enkirra spread his hands slowly, conjuring a broad pane of light, and with a single practiced curve of the flat of his hand, he honed it to a sword's edge. Incandescent blade in hand, he approached the monster and laid an almost tender hand upon its head, stroking one of its yellowed horns.

So it ends at last, the Apsu whispered.

Enkirra nodded, almost with deference. "You were a worthy foe."

The sword of light flashed up—a hot knife through scaled and ridged butter. The Apsu's eyes bolted open, then its head and long neck separated and splashed into the waters.

"Now the Deep, and everything on either side of it, belongs to me."

A collective tremor passed through every cluster of humanity, in every corner and cranny of the earth. Intensified in the manic lust of rutting bodies, woken in their beds from the fever-dreams of some imagined doom, or an involuntary shiver dismissed as some vague, foolish dread, all sensed something had changed—some fundamental fact. A whirlwind on the horizon, an eclipsing of their collective suns.

Oh, what a glorious age it would be.

About the Author:

Marcus Turner is a speculative, horror, and dark fantasy author from Melbourne, Australia, where he lives with his wife Tita and his two children. He was first published in Deadset Press' 'Beginnings' anthology with his story, A Spark of Youth, *in November 2018, and has since been featured in several other anthologies. He is a keen gamer, metalhead, avid reader of Batman and Judge Dredd comics, and is a little more obsessed with Cthulhu and all things Cthulhu Mythos than is probably healthy. Marcus cites Clive Barker, Stephen King, H.P. Lovecraft, Edgar Allen Poe, George R.R. Martin and R. Scott Bakker as the major influences on his own writing. He currently working on his first novel, entitled* Land of the Righteous. *You can connect with him via the following media:*

Facebook: www.facebook.com/MarcusTurnerWriter/
Twitter: @FuryThePhoenix
Instagram: @marcusturnerauthor
Website: marcusturnerauthor.com

COMMANDER

Sam M. Phillips

Strong prototype,
Phoenix rising,
Sizing up the ship
As we slip
Through the black hole,
I feel a tear
In my soul,
Wear courage like a badge
As we drive a wedge
Through reality,
You have this ability,
The agility
Of your mind
As you find
A path for us to wind
Through this dense matter,
You never let
Your energy scatter,
I need to get

Out of your way,
You need room to play
With the fine pieces,
Your energy never ceases,
Space-time creases
Around the ship
And we all lose grip
On reality
As you continue
To be able
To handle
This swirling change,
Nothing strange
To you,
You're the ship's commander,
And this is just what you do.

About the Author:

Sam M. Phillips is the co-founder of Zombie Pirate Publishing, producing short story anthologies and helping -emerging writers. His own work has appeared in dozens of anthologies and magazines such as Full Metal Horror and World War Four. He recently published his debut novella, SCIENCE FICTION DOUBLE FEATURE: Phosphorus & Into The Eye, *available now!*

He lives in northern New South Wales, Australia, and enjoys reading, walking, and playing drums in the death metal band Decryptus. He is also a prolific poet and his poetry can be read on his blog **www.bigconfusingwords.wordpress.com**

CAPRICORN'S RETURN

Austin P. Sheehan

As stasis pod 182 opened, Eshan fell to the cold steel floor. Breathing deeply, he smiled as he heard the moans and coughs of the other colonists. He was finally home. A hand reached out to help him up as he got to his knees, moving his weak and aching limbs for the first time in decades.

"Welcome to Nashira. Are you okay?" asked a brunette in a pale blue shipsuit.

"Never been better," he said, taking her warm hand and staggering to his feet. He looked into her brown eyes and tried to think of something to say, his head still foggy after being in stasis for so long.

"I'm medical officer Dorn. If you start feeling sick, come find me in the Medbay. For now, get dressed." She nodded towards his locker, "then follow the others to the mess."

Eshan pulled out a dull orange shipsuit from the locker. It was nothing special: a 'Capricornus Expedition' patch on one sleeve—a creature straight out of ancient myth, half-goat and half-fish—and '182' on the other. He pulled it on, leaning against the stasis pod for balance, his weak limbs protesting. With his stomach growling for food, Eshan staggered down the clean and brightly lit hallway to the mess, amidst a sea of other orange-clad figures.

"So, Number 182, what's your story?" asked a man next to him as he waited, tray in hand, for his meal.

"I'm Eshan, from Tychoe colony, Sirius," he replied, looking the man up and down, noting the 103 sewn onto his sleeve, cropped sandy hair and weathered face.

"I'm Marlowe from Adhara," said the man, holding out his hand. "But these days you can call me Colonist 103." The men exchanged smiles as Ehsan clasped the older man's strong hand in his own. Taking their meals—regulation meat and vegetable stew with bread rolls—they found seats at one of the many crowded tables, the large windowless room full of colour, noise and warmth.

"Good slop," said Colonist 157 as he made room for Eshan. "Best meal I've had in fifty years!"

Eshan smiled at the joke as he sat down. "I'm Eshan, and this is Marlowe," he said, tearing off a piece of his bread roll.

"Hollister," said 157 with a broad grin, showing off his yellow teeth. "Nice to meet you."

"Why did you sign up for the expedition, Hollister?" asked Marlowe as Eshan savoured the sensation of having real food in his mouth. He leaned back in his chair with a smile. This was his first meal with his new family. He and these two-hundred-and-forty-nine people were going to build a whole new colony together.

The sounds of conversation and the scrape of cutlery on plates ceased as a handful of blue-suited figures entered the mess.

"Here we go," said Hollister with a wry smile, running his hands through his dark hair. "Time for the mission briefing."

"On behalf of ColVentures, welcome to Nashira!" boomed a man with cropped grey hair. He was met with a round of hearty applause from the colonists. "I'm Kiernan, the overseer of the Capricornus Expedition. Together, we're going to turn this planet into the next Centauri."

Eshan grinned eagerly, glancing between Hollister and Marlowe, excitement welling inside him.

"As you know, Nashira is a mineral-rich planet, right in the H-zone of Gamma Capricorni. We expect Nashira to become a major trading colony, and it all starts with the efforts of you brave men and women, and not to mention the crew of the *Panthea* who brought us all this way!"

Another round of applause.

"I'm Captain Triggs," announced a tall dark woman, standing next to Kiernan.

Eshan sat on the edge of his seat, captivated by her jet black hair and her proud, welcoming smile.

"On behalf of the crew of the *Panthea*, I hope you had a satisfactory journey."

A round of laughter and applause followed her statement.

"My ship and my crew will remain with you on Nashira until we are relieved by the *Panthea II* in approximately five years," she continued, her voice serious. "Until the colony has been built, you will eat, sleep and socialise on board. Embedded into your shipsuit is an access pass—" she gestured to the cuff of her light blue sleeve— "allowing you to access your assigned quarters on level G. Some areas—the mess, the observation decks, the sanitary quarters, the medbays—are accessible to everyone. However, you will not have access to the *Panthea*'s bridge, the crew's quarters, armoury or engineering bay."

"How long until the colony's ready, Captain?" asked a man with a dark moustache sitting a few metres from where Kiernan and Triggs stood.

"If everything goes to plan, we expect it to be ready in a matter of weeks," she said, glancing at Kiernan who nodded in confirmation.

A tentative hand inched into the air at the next table, and a soft voice asked, "Why is the *Panthea* staying so long?"

Eshan leaned to the left to see who asked the question, catching only a glimpse of long blonde hair.

"Good question, Colonist 62," Captain Triggs said, pausing until she had everyone's attention. "This is important, so listen up. One reason we are staying is in case things don't go to plan. If disaster strikes, if the colony's dome is breached, everyone must return to the *Panthea*."

"Captain Triggs is right," said Kiernan, stepping forward. "Never forget that the Nashiran air is toxic, and breathing it is likely to result in severe sickness, if not death. Until the dome has been sealed, pressurised and purified, keep your EVA suits on, your helmets and gloves sealed tight at all times while in the cargo bay and when you're out on the surface."

"What do you reckon?" Marlowe asked, after the briefing was over.

"I'm just happy to be here, to have somewhere to call home," said Eshan, with a relaxed smile. After years of jumping from one planet to another, he was finally where he belonged.

"We've gotta build it first, 182," said Hollister, leaning back in his hair, hands behind his head.

"They make it sound romantic," Marlowe added, a note of concern in his voice. "But being the first colonists on a planet is a tough gig, Eshan. You know we've got a shit-ton of hard work ahead of us, yeah?"

"A shit-ton of highly paid work!" said Hollister, giving Eshan a friendly elbow to the ribs. "Most of the hard work is done by servodroids these days, so even a softie like 182 here will be fine."

"I know what I've signed up for," he replied, giving them both a knowing smile. "I'm not afraid of a hard day's work." Eshan didn't mind Hollister's digs, that's what friends do. For the first time in his life, he felt accepted. He knew he was going to like it here.

"Out with it then," said Marlowe, following Eshan up the stairs to the H-deck Observation Room.

"Out with what?"

"You still haven't told me why you left Tychoe, why you signed up to be a colonist."

"No reason," said Eshan, trying to evade the question, only wanting to look out over the planet that they were going to call home.

"I don't buy that. No-way would anyone pack up their life, say goodbye to everyone they knew, and risk it all to come out to some barren rock for no bloody reason."

Eshan had stopped listening. He had reached the thick window and was staring out at the Nashiran surface. "It's beautiful . . ." he said, taking it in. Lit faintly by a distant star, the planet's rough dark surface was bathed in a cool glow, a row of jagged mountains in the distance. In his mind's eye, he saw how their home would look. The rectangular grey and orange buildings he saw half a century ago in the ColVentures office, arranged just so, under a clear dome.

"It'll do," replied Marlowe with a shrug. "Come on, let's find our quarters."

"I'll catch up with you, okay?" said Eshan, still mesmerised by what he saw out the window.

Eshan dredged through his memories, recalling his time on other colonies. Amongst the mass of humanity spread across the Sol, Wolf, Centauri, and Sirius systems, he'd always been an outsider. As hard as he tried, he never fit in. He had travelled from city to city, planet to planet, looking for somewhere where he felt he belonged. For years he couldn't tell whether he was called on by destiny, or if he was somehow exiled from humanity, somehow cursed to never find somewhere he could call home. His heart swelled with joy as he looked out over the barren planet. *There has to be a place for you in a colony that you helped to build.* He sighed, content in the knowledge that his long, lonely journey was finally at an end.

"Attention colonists," boomed a voice over the ship's intercom. "Kiernan here. If you want to be one of the first to set foot on Nashira, report to the mess immediately for tomorrow's mission."

Eshan's heart leapt. This was an opportunity he didn't want to miss.

Blackness. The twinkling constellation of Capricornus appeared in the darkness. Rushing towards it, towards Gamma Capricorni, Eshan felt like he was falling. Faster and faster he fell, and soon the planet Nashira appeared—first as a speck, then it grew larger and larger. A giant triangle appeared below him, etched deeply into the planet's rough surface. In the middle of the triangle was the circle of the colony's dome, and it grew as he kept falling towards it, faster and faster. Helpless against forces he could not see, that he could not understand, he smashed into the dome's impregnable surface.

Eshan woke from his dream with a groan. Stiff and sore, he rolled out of his bunk, looking at the light grey walls of his almost featureless quarters. Next to the steel door was a clock and a map of the *Panthea*. Below the map was his small brown trunk, containing all his personal effects: clothes, shoes, his digital library of books, films and music, and two bottles of Tychoe whisky which he was looking forward to sharing with Hollister and Marlowe after the colony had been built. The clock read 0500—*why was he up so early?* Then he remembered. He was going to be one of the first humans to set foot on the Nashiran surface. Trembling with excitement, he pulled on his shipsuit, thinking of the future, of the colony that he and his family would build together. Maybe they'd even put up a plaque of the first colonists to walk on the surface. This was where it all started. But first, breakfast.

Eshan met the other eleven volunteers for the first mission in the mess. Marlowe greeted him with a friendly nod, and with breakfast tray in hand, Eshan joined the group.

"Good morning," he said, nodding to Marlowe as he put his tray down, a broad smile on his face. Today was going to be a good day.

"Excellent, it looks like everyone is here," said Kiernan, following Eshan to the table.

"Good morning, sir," replied a blonde woman, the number 62 embroidered into her orange ship-suit.

"Good morning," Kiernan replied.

"It's June," Colonist 62 said, blushing, looking down at what remained of her breakfast.

"Nice to meet you, June. Just between us, I'd rather call you all by your names, but 250 people—not including the crew—is an awful lot to remember. So," he continued, rubbing his hands together, "is everyone excited to get out on the surface?"

Everyone nodded, smiling at each other with nervous anticipation.

"What can you tell us about Nashira, sir?" asked Colonist 115, a bearded man, old but tough looking, who sat opposite Eshan.

"Good question. Firstly, Nashira's an old planet. This system is millions of years older than anything we've colonised yet. Thousands of years ago she may have been lush, full of plant and animal life," Kiernan said, his eyes alive with excitement. "There's still moisture in her thin atmosphere, some sparse vegetation still clings to life on the surface, and there are several large bodies of water."

"Any chance of intelligent life?" asked Eshan, captivated.

"No," said Kiernan, with a firm shake of his head. "But as soon as the colony's been established, I'm going to take a team out exploring. A planet this old has got to have secrets, even if they're buried beneath the ground or at the bottom of the sea." Marlowe and Eshan exchanged smiles and nodded, both determined to do whatever they could to be a part of Kiernan's team.

After a safety briefing and donning their EVA suits, Eshan, Marlowe and the rest of the volunteers gathered around Kiernan in the *Panthea's* vast cargo bay. Rows of rust-coloured heavy terraforming vehicles, small silver transports and an array of machinery lined the two walls, and Eshan kept looking towards the wall where 'CARGO BAY DOOR 01' was painted in bold black letters. This was his first time in an EVA suit, and he was struggling, sweating and panting after just stumbling the ten metres to where the rest of the colonists stood.

"The suits are a pain in the arse, aren't they?" said Kiernan over the radio, and Eshan could hear the smile in his voice.

"Sir, how are we going to get any work done?" asked Colonist 89, a woman with dark messy curls. "How are we going to build the colony wearing these? I can hardly walk!"

"We've got—shit, get out of the way!" yelled Kiernan, raising his arm and pointing behind Eshan.

Oh shit, he thought, taking an awkward half step, twisting and turning in his suit to see what was behind him. His stomach turned to water. The white arm of a construction crane sliced through the air towards him. His heart pounding, Eshan tried to move. But his legs, trapped in the heavy EVA suit, weren't responding. Screams filled his radio earpiece as the impact came, throwing orange figures across the floor of the cargo bay. A steel beam crushed Eshan's right side, his arm, his leg. He screamed out at the piercing agony consumed him. While Kiernan called for a medic, Marlowe crawled across the floor toward him. Eshan looked at the proudly painted cargo bay door, at an orange-gloved hand reaching for him—everything slowly fading from his grasp.

He sat on a red chair. On the other side of the table sat a man with a neat solver beard and sharp-looking grey suit. "Where am I?" Eshan wanted to ask, but his mouth wouldn't respond.

"Welcome to ColVentures, Eshan Suintler. I'm Sevan Buckinger. Tell me, why do you want to join the Capricornus expedition?" The room slowly faded away.

A slow, gentle beeping roused him. But then it stopped, and then there was nothing but silence. Silence and darkness.

Below the red chair was grey carpet, perfectly clean. Pictures of spaceships and planets hung on a white wall. Through a window to the left, Eshan watched a red sun slowly fall towards a cluster of tall buildings.

"The adventure, the opportunity to be part of something special," he said, turning to face Buckinger. "To help build a new colony from the ground up." *The words came out of Eshan's mouth, but he didn't want to say them.*

The beeping came again, faster this time. An image. A dark red triangle. A beeping red triangle, getting fainter and fainter.

There was a model on the table. Tiny grey and orange buildings, neatly arranged under a dome. Everything was in its place, just the way he liked it.

"We've checked your records, Eshan. You're a hard worker, you've no criminal convictions," said Buckinger, before hesitating. "But you've moved around a lot, not sticking at the same job or staying on the one planet for any longer than two years. That's a concern."

Pain shot through Eshan's body. He screamed, his ragged voice echoing around the room, louder than the incessant beeps. Louder than the triangles. Then the beeps changed, and his pain eased.

The red sun had not hit the buildings yet, but Eshan was sure they would soon.

"As a colonist," continued the grey man, "you'll have to stay on for a minimum of five years." *Those words sparked something in Eshan, and he turned back to Buckinger. He had known this moment was coming. Had he foreseen it, or did he remember it?*

"I've never felt at home anywhere before," *his mouth answered as if controlled by someone else, while Eshan's fingers traced a triangle around the colony.* "I've never felt like I belonged. But I know I'll feel at home somewhere I've built *with my own two hands. I know that I'll find my place in Capricornus. Don't worry about me, sir. I'm not going to come back!" Eshan tapped the glass dome between them to emphasise his conviction.*

"Very well," said Buckinger, apparently satisfied with his response. Eshan looked again at the pictures on the wall. Had they changed? Or had they always been goat-headed fish?

As he opened his eyes, Eshan knew he wasn't in Buckinger's office anymore. Turning his head from side to side, he saw slate-grey steel walls above the glass sides of his medpod and dim blue lights from empty medpods. It was silent aside from an intermittent low beeping. *Medpods? I'm in the medbay? What happ—*

Memories came flooding back; the crane arm swinging towards him, the screams filling his radio. Marlowe's gloved hand. *Where is everyone?* Eshan tried to explore the medpod with his hands, but his right arm wouldn't move. His left arm flailed weakly, finding nothing against the smooth clear surface.

"Doctor? Medic?" he yelled with the last of his strength. "Is there anyone there?" Nothing. Just a quickening of the medpod's beeping as drowsiness overcame him.

When he regained consciousness, Eshan managed to lift his head. Still no sign of anyone else. *How long have I been here?* Looking down at his body, his right leg and right arm were in fibreglass casts. He ran his left hand down his chest, feeling his ribs through the thin blue medrobe. Flexing his fingers and toes, his arms and legs, Eshan's weak, unused muscles ached. There were flashes of pain, but it was manageable. When he tried to sit upright, his muscles protested and a wave of nausea overcame him, accompanied by a fast-paced beeping. Eshan lay back in the medpod. *Where was everyone?* The medbay doors were sealed. He needed to get out of here. He needed to find Marlowe and the rest of the colonists.

Eshan sat up slowly, pushing down the nausea, ignoring the pain. Experimenting with his right arm, tensing it, moving it as much as he could within the confines of the cast, he felt that the bones had healed—*I must have been here for weeks!* Nearby was a trolley with cutting implements: scissors, scalpels, and a short saw, each shining in the bright lights. Eshan grabbed the scalpel and worked the blade between his delicate skin and the cast, then pushed down. The scalpel dug into his skin—the sharp blade sliced through his flesh, and he felt the warm trickle of blood against his skin. Gritting his teeth, fighting against the pain, against the nausea, he pressed on. Covered in sweat, his arm dripping blood, Eshan sighed as the fibreglass cast fell to the floor. With the last of his strength, Eshan cut strips from the bottom of his medrobe and wound them around his arm to stop the bleeding.

Laying back down, as weariness overcame him, Eshan tensed his right leg to see if that too had healed. Pain shot up his spine to his skull. It hadn't healed, but he needed to get out of here. He needed to find the rest of the crew, the rest of his family. The medpod's beeping intensified, then cut out as a clear fluid travelled down one of the various tubes, then into his veins. The pain was disappearing. With his consciousness ebbing away, Eshan saw a pair of crutches stowed under the pod beside him.

The next time he woke, Eshan unplugged the tubes connecting him to the medpod, slung his legs over the side and, with a deep breath, tested them on the cold steel floor. Pain shot through his right knee, but he had to keep going. He had to find someone. He had to find his family. Supporting himself on his left leg, he hopped forward until he reached the cool surface of the other medpod. Reaching down, he grabbed the crutches, secured them under each arm, and smiled. He could do this. After catching his breath, he made his way to the medbay doors. Sensing his presence, they slid open with a hiss, revealing an empty hallway with flickering lights.

"Hello?" Silence. No, not silence. Nothingness. As if all normally unnoticed noises; the hum of the ship's air conditioning and life support systems, suddenly ceased. It was like someone had heard him, and had decided not to reply.

Sweating, anxious, and feeling even more alone than ever before, Eshan hobbled down the dark hallway. Hunger gnawed at his insides, compelling him to seek the mess. He needed food, he needed to find the other colonists. If anyone was still on board, they'd go to the mess to eat. He turned down a well-lit hallway, looking through windows into darkened rooms. No movement. No noise. *Where was everyone? Had they all moved to the colony?* Oh no. He stopped dead in the hallway, his heart sinking as he rested on his crutches. *Had he missed the chance to build somewhere he could call home?* With a pit of dread and hopelessness inside him, he pushed on, hearing only his panting and the tapping of his crutches on the steel floor.

At the doorway to the *Panthea*'s mess, Eshan waved his hand over the sensor to open the door. Sliding open with a hiss, they revealed nothing but darkness. The lights were out. The illumination from the hallway showed an unexpected emptiness. *Where were the tables and chairs?* As he breathed in, a faint odour tainted the air, something off. His gut tightened. Something was wrong. As his eyes adjusted, Eshan stepped further into the darkness. In the middle of the room, in the middle of the long and terrible silence, Eshan made out a dark shape. A pyramid, built from upturned tables, their thin steel legs raised to the sky as if in prayer. The hairs rose on the back of his neck—there was something very, very wrong here. As he approached the looming shape, the smell became rank; so sharp and bitter that his eyes watered. It entered his nose, his mouth, working its way through him, violating him, making him retch.

Eshan held his breath as he crept closer to the pyramid and noticed dark, twisted shapes wrapped around the table legs. The floor was cold, slick, and sticky under his feet. Eshan stopped, as if his body knew not to go any further. With a click the lights came on, blinding him with the sudden brightness. The pyramid of tables was dark red with blood. *What the hell?* Eshan's heart lurched in his chest. *Oh no.* The bodies of countless crew and colonists wearing torn and shredded orange and blue shipsuits were impaled on the table legs. *Shit.* Their arms, their legs and heads had been torn off. *Oh God.* Their stomachs were ripped open, entrails hanging down to the blood-covered floor, where a pile of arms and legs, torn flesh and bone gleamed in the light. *Fuck no!* Staggering backwards, away from the horrific sight, Eshan slipped in a pool of drying blood. He fell, his crutches sliding out from underneath him, and his body crashed to the floor. Shaking in fear, agony and revulsion he threw up, emptying what little was in his stomach over the floor and his bloodstained medrobe.

Backing away from the gore, dragging his leg behind him, Eshan saw images painted in blood on the mess' pale walls. Swirls like waves, triangles and eyeless faces. But he couldn't look away from the dominating image, a monster with a long-horned head, equine forelegs and a long body that somehow twisted into the grotesque finned tail of a fish. Gathering himself together, he groped for a way out of this nightmare.

Behind him, the door to the galley beckoned. Eshan slid

across the floor. Grabbing his crutches, he pulled himself to his feet, his legs aching, his arms shaking. He glanced back at the pyramid of horror as the lights winked out. Trying not to think, trying not to scream, he entered the galley. The floor was littered with pre-prepped food containers. With the sour taste of bile still in his mouth, Eshan didn't want food anymore, but his body urged him on, compelled him towards the wall of freezers and fridges. Amongst the walk-in fridges he found a handful of protein bars which he shoved into the pockets of his shipsuit, trying to calm his racing heart. *What the hell had happened?*

Eshan hobbled down a dark empty hallway, icy rivulets of cold sweat running down his back. *What had happened? Who or what had torn those people apart—and where were they now?* All he knew was that he needed to find the armoury. He didn't want to be unarmed if he found whatever had torn the other colonists apart—or if it found him. Every five metres he paused for breath, looking up and down the dark hallways, listening for any noise, any hint of another being on board the *Panthea*.

He stumbled upon a stairway with a sign 'TO OBSERVATION DECK' and turned towards it. Stairs were hard on crutches, with his right leg still in its fibreglass prison, but Eshan needed to see the colony. He needed to know if there was anyone still alive. Covered in sweat and blood, with his chest heaving and his body aching, he finally made it. The thick windows of the observation deck let in the last of the pale blue-pink rays from Gamma Capricorni, going down behind the mountains, a row of jagged triangles in the distance. Before him was the colony, the place that should have been his home. His heart sank. The colony should have been well-lit, but the only light came from the distant sun. The buildings were in disarray, either destroyed or still under construction. In the centre of the dome, a grotesque structure made out of the cannibalised walls and ceilings of other buildings towered over the ruins. Looking up at the dome, Eshan collapsed to the ground in horror. Two gaping holes had been smashed into the dome, letting toxic Nashiran air into the colony—and who knew what else? Succumbing to his despair and loneliness, Eshan looked up into the alien sky, silent tears streaming down his face. He might be the only one left alive on this godless rock.

I can't do this! he thought, beating his fists on the cold unforgiving floor. *This is not what I signed up for, dammit!* He cried, wracked with fear and hopelessness. He was meant to build not just a new colony with these people, but a new home, a new life. Now he would have to bury them—if he survived. Choking down a protein bar, he considered his options. He wouldn't know if he really was alone until he'd explored every room of the massive colony ship. Maybe some of the crew were still alive. Maybe they could fly this cursed craft back home. But he was getting ahead of himself. He needed a gun, something to defend himself with. But even if he found the armoury, he couldn't get in without the right access chip. Hell, he couldn't even return to his own quarters without his shipsuit, which was hopefully still in the medbay. And he would not explore the ship any further unarmed. Swallowing ragged breaths of air, trying to calm his thumping heart, Eshan realised what he had to do.

Shaking with adrenaline and exhaustion, Eshan stumbled down hallway after hallway, back to familiar ground. Then he froze, his blood turning to ice. The light grey walls of the well-lit hallway had been defaced. Someone or something had been here recently. *Shit.* And whoever it was had left him a message. A message written in blood. Slick smears of blood making out sixteen tall letters, each reaching the roof. Eshan couldn't look away as the ragged letters merged into four simple words. BEHOLD. YOUR. NEW. GOD.

Who wrote this? Eshan held his breath, looking up and down the hallway. Nothing. No noise. No footprints. Eshan swallowed hard. He had to keep going, he needed to get to the armoury more than ever. Taking a deep breath, fighting every instinct he had, he moved forward, the tapping of his crutches echoing down the steel hallway.

He peered into the darkness of the mess, trying not to breathe in the foul stench. The pyramid of bodies was still there. There was no sound, no movement, so he cautiously edged closer towards the grotesque scene. The lights began flickering, shedding unwanted light on the carnage, on the desecrated bodies of his friends, his family. His gaze was constantly drawn to the horrific scene, but what he was looking for was on the floor. His heart in his mouth, Eshan used his crutches to search through a pile of bloody orange-clad limbs, knocking the ones on top aside so he could see what was beneath them. He tried not to look at the numbers on the sleeves, but couldn't look away when an arm with the number 157 fell at his feet. *Shit, Hollister. You didn't deserve this.* Gritting his teeth in determination, he pushed aside another leg to reveal what he needed. An arm in a pale blue sleeve. Reaching down, he picked up his disgusting prize, the revulsion rising within him, making him retch. He tried not to see that the flesh of the hand had been torn off, revealing thin skeletal bones. Closing his eyes, Eshan gripped the sleeve of the shipsuit and shook until the arm slid out and landed on the floor with a wet, heavy *thunk.*

Eshan made his way towards the door, trying not to think

about the horror and the pain that his fellow colonists had endured. Something made him stop. A sound. A word. A thought. Had he missed something? He paused, leaning on his crutches and turned around, surveying the scene for what he hoped would be the last time. Bodies on the tables. Blood, arms and legs on the floor. Then it hit him—*the heads! Where were their heads?* Eshan scrambled to the exit, closing the mess door behind him, and slid down to the floor, his chest heaving with his deep breaths, his arms and legs trembling with exertion.

After drawing in several harsh, painful breaths, Eshan tied the blue shipsuit sleeve to his crutches, then pulled himself to his feet. He needed to find a weapon. Looking down the hallway to the right, then to the left, Eshan groaned, realising he had no idea where the armoury was. He needed a map, and the only map he could remember seeing was on the wall in his quarters. *Shit.* He needed his shipsuit to get into his quarters, so he had to return to the medbay.

His chest tight with icy dread, Eshan staggered down the hallway towards the medbay. For the past hour, he had heard nothing but his own haggard breathing, the tapping and scraping of his crutches on the cold steel floor. But he could feel that he was being followed. He could feel eyes bearing into the back of his neck, burrowing into his skin. But when he turned, nothing. He was alone with his fear, wandering the endless hallways of the *Panthea*. Eshan was past breaking point. Whenever he closed his eyes, the shredded bodies of his friends filled his head, the ropes of intestines hanging from their desecrated corpses, the floor covered with legs and arms torn out of their sockets. *What happened?* he asked himself for the hundredth time. *Who tore them apart? Where were their heads?* As he staggered forward, another question hit him. *What had smashed the colony dome?*

Reaching the medbay, Eshan opened the door and stepped inside. His hair stood on end, his blood was frozen in his veins. Something was different. As he saw it, his stomach turned to ice—an image had been painted above his medpod, still slick with wet blood. A horned goat head, inverted triangles where its eyes should be, connected to a twisting fish tail. Gasping for air, Eshan looked down at his medpod. Another blood-soaked arm was waiting for him, still wrapped in a pale blue shipsuit, proudly bearing the Capricornus Expedition patch above the letters M.O. DORN. His heart sank as he recognised the name. The pretty medical officer who helped him when they first arrived on Nashira. Behind him, the medbay door hissed shut. *He was not alone.* Too scared to move, Eshan tried to swallow, then tried to pray. A voice filled the room—or his head—he couldn't tell the difference.

"This planet . . . not Godless after all." The voice was a deep guttural rumble, echoing up from the floor and reverberating through his spine. His body moved without his control, without his consent. Like a machine, Eshan grabbed the arm in the medpod, his crutches clattering to the floor. Helpless to resist the commands he received, Eshan pirouetted 180 degrees on his broken leg, bowed, and collapsed in agony, still grasping the blood-soaked arm.

"Don't be afraid . . . Eshan. There is a place for you here . . . with us."

Eshan tried to block out the deep dark voice, tried to keep his eyes focused on the closed doorway, but couldn't. His head lifted, his eyes focusing on a pair of dark feet, caked in black, drying blood. *Oh no.* He tried to fight it, tried to look away, but his gaze travelled up the legs, still wearing a stained and shredded pale blue shipsuit. Above the waist, the shipsuit was torn open, revealing scarred skin with fresh blood dripping down the emaciated stomach. Eshan tried to close his eyes, tried to blink, but his gaze held firm. An inverted triangle had been raggedly cut from the sternum up through the soft fatty flesh of what had been a pair of small, dark breasts. Torn and flayed skin hung loosely from the deep wound, pale ribs visible through the streams of thick dark blood. Eshan tried to scream but couldn't, his voice died away as his eyes rose ever upwards.

"On behalf of the crew . . . we hope you enjoy . . . your stay." Her lips had been ripped off, exposing a mouth full of broken teeth, fixed in a grotesque grin. Blood dripped down her cheeks, onto her chest. Captain Triggs' bottom eyelids had been cut out, leaving two red triangles of raw flesh. Her eyes were dead; lifeless pale orbs. But behind them was a wild energy, controlling Eshan, staring into the lonely depths of his soul.

"You have been chosen . . . to bear witness . . . to the wrath of the exiled God."

A vision appeared in Eshan's mind, the *Panthea* returning to Adhara, to the human colonies. Dragged behind the colony ship came an unstoppable darkness, an unspeakable cruelty, an unimaginable horror.

"Join us in . . . the beginning . . . of the Great Devouring."

No! Too late, Eshan understood why he held Medical Officer Dorn's arm in his trembling hands. He tried to scream, tried to fight the commands his body received with all his strength. But nothing could stop his hands from slowly and reverently raising the bloody piece of meat to his face.

About the Author:

Austin P. Sheehan is a writer of speculative fiction, a lover of language, literature and '90s TV. Armed with a psychology degree, he went out into the world to further study humanity, and now prefers the company of his wife and greyhounds.

*Austin grew up in Victoria's high country, and despite living in Melbourne for ten years, still feels at home amongst the mountains. In fact, you'll often find mountains in his stories, whether they are science fiction, fantasy, alternative history or horror. If you want to discover what secrets are hidden in the mountains, go to **www.austinpsheehan.com** or find him on twitter @AustinPSheehan.*

Austin's novella Submerged City - *part of Aussie Speculative Fiction's 'Drowned Earth' series - was published in 2019. His short stories have been published in 'Beginnings' and 'Journeys' (Deadset Press) and 'A Bond of Words' (Scout Media), and his microfiction appears in 'Curses & Cauldrons' (Blood Song Books) and the 'Worlds' 'Monsters' and 'Apocalypse' anthologies by Black Hare Press.*

THE CAPRICORN TRIAL

Alanah Andrews

"Next up, meet the hot contenders for this year's Zodiac Trials."

Xanthe paused in the midst of making a peanut butter sandwich, then turned towards the flickering wall-screen just visible in the adjoining living room. The familiar musical introduction filtered through the small apartment, wrapping around her throat like a noose as the butter knife trembled in her hand.

"Good morning, Australia!" said the ever-cheery host of the Zodiac Show, Greyson Jones. He was dressed in his signature outfit—a close-fitting suit cut in the latest style—while his tie matched the crimson colour of the tag in Xanthe's ear. "I know, I know, it seems like only yesterday that we farewelled the last group off our screens and into society, but my calendar tells me that it's time to start the excitement all over again. I'm certain that you are just going to *love* our contenders this year."

Xanthe moved towards the wall-screen in a trance, knife

gripped tightly in her hand while the peanut butter sandwich lay forgotten on the bench. Images of contenders from the last Zodiac Trials swirled together on the giant studio screens behind Greyson. Their faces were all instantly recognisable to Xanthe—to most of Australia—after dominating the news forums and gracing their wall-screens for the better part of twelve months. There was Nikita. Lillian. Jordan C. Jordan F— better known as *The Beast*. Rick, Cameron, and little Sophie who nobody had seriously thought would make it past the Capricorn Trial, let alone all twelve.

Xanthe sat on the faded couch in the living room as the winners from the previous year were displayed triumphantly, waving out at her from the screen. As she watched, trying to calm her racing heart, the images melted away to show Greyson shaking hands and posing with a group of people unfamiliar to Xanthe.

"I've spent the past three weeks travelling to some of the top Zodiac Schools in the country," the host explained. "And I know that I say this every year, but we really are spoilt for choice."

The video was replaced by a giant collage of faces, and Xanthe peered into the mass, wondering if she could find her own blue eyes staring nervously back at her.

"Tonight, on the eve of this year's Capricorn Trial, do I have a treat for you." Greyson flashed his perfect white teeth. "Ten of our top contenders are with me right here in the studio."

The studio audience cheered as the camera panned across to the right, where a group of young adults sat perched on chairs against a wall like they were in a firing line. Xanthe noted their athletic builds, their composure as the camera zoomed in on one after the other. One boy flexed his arm and pointed at his muscles. Was he really that confident, or was it all put on for show?

"First up, I'd like you to meet Natasha," said Greyson, and the camera focussed on a girl at the end of the line. Her dark hair was straight, flowing over her shoulders like a pristine waterfall, hiding the tag in her ear.

"So tell me, Natasha," said the host, with a smile that was almost genuine, "you're a five-times national gymnastics champion?"

"Six," Natasha corrected him, and Xanthe knew the mistake hadn't been an accident—this was all rehearsed to show off the prowess of Greyson's predicted winners. "And once I pass the Zodiac Trials and the travel restrictions are dropped, I'm going to go on to be the world champion." The crowd clapped and cheered, the low rumble making Xanthe's stomach clench.

"Would you like to show us some of your moves?"

The girl rose elegantly to her feet. Turning to the audience, she gave a little bow and then performed a flawless routine involving somersaults and handsprings that left Xanthe feeling dizzy.

"Impressive," said Greyson, continuing to clap long after the audience had ceased. "Really, very impressive. I can tell you're going to be a formidable force in tomorrow's Trial." He turned to the audience. "Natasha Lawrence, everyone—she'll be one to watch out for."

As Greyson began introducing the next contender, Xanthe switched off the wall-screen, breathing heavily. Her hands shook, and as she walked back into the kitchen and placed the knife on the bench, she told herself in no uncertain terms to calm the fuck down. She glanced over at the glowing digits on the oven clock. Her parents would be finished work in a little over an hour, so she just had to keep her mind busy for—

A loud pulse of music made her jump. She gave a little

laugh that sounded strange in the empty kitchen, then glanced at the caller ID on her phone. All week, people had been on tenterhooks, their eyes drawn to the crimson tag in her ear, and she didn't think she could deal with another awkward conversation where *good luck* sounded more like *goodbye*. But the boy who was calling was someone she was always happy to talk to. The red tag in Aidan's ear meant that at least *his* voice wouldn't be filled with pity like the others.

"Hey," she said into the receiver.

"Hey to you too," said Aidan. "Are you watching the Zodiac Show?"

Xanthe returned to the living room, lying down on the couch and trying to relax. "Just turned it off. It gave me the creeps."

"Yeah, I know what you mean. But did you see that Roland was on there?"

"Who?" asked Xanthe.

"Roland. You remember, from high school? He got a scholarship in Year Eight to attend one of the Zodiac Schools over west. Capricorn-3, I think."

"Mmmm I think I vaguely remember," said Xanthe, casting her mind back over the haze of the last six years. "Good for him—I'd much rather that someone with actual work ethic and talent went to those schools than the ones who only got in because mummy and daddy could afford it."

Aidan didn't laugh. "You don't think that rich kids put in effort?"

Xanthe bit her tongue. "Don't get all defensive. I'm sure that Tabitha works really hard—"

"She does—"

"—I'm just saying that kids in our school worked hard too."

Aidan snorted, and Xanthe felt herself bristle.

"What, just 'cause you're dating some blue tag from

Aquarius-2, you've suddenly forgotten which side of the maglev tracks you were raised on?"

"Some blue tag?" Aidan's voice grew louder. "Xanthe, I know you're scared about tomorrow, but don't take that out on me. Tab's lovely, okay—and you know it."

Xanthe became aware of her hand gripping the edge of the couch and she ordered herself to let go. Taking a deep breath, she stood up, walking back into the kitchen.

"I'm sorry, okay. It's just . . ."

"I know."

There was silence as Xanthe leaned heavily against the kitchen bench, thinking about what waited for her the next day. She counted each breath as it filled her lungs. *One. Two. Don't say it.* "Do you ever think that maybe . . ."

"Maybe what, Xanthe?"

Three. Four. Small voice. "Maybe they should have kept the Restricted Birth Policy in place."

Aidan was quiet on the other end of the line. "Neither of us would have been born if that was the case," he said at last. "Neither of our parents would have qualified for a reproductive pass."

"Maybe that would have been better." She tapped a fingernail on the stained bench.

"Really, Xanthe?" said Aidan. "Were the last twenty years so terrible? I seem to remember that we had some pretty good times together."

Xanthe felt herself flush. "But tomorrow—"

"Reproduction is a right, Xanthe. *Life* is a right. But overpopulation is a real issue. Under the old rules, our parents wouldn't have been allowed to have children. Ever. You can't tell a person that they can't have kids."

"Can't you? You sound like our old teachers. Or Greyson."

"Thanks." Aidan's voice was wry. "Look, you and I know

that it's better to have lived for twenty years than to have never lived at all. Go ahead and pass the twelve trials and then come up with a better solution for overpopulation, okay?"

Xanthe picked up the sandwich and took a bite. It felt dry in her mouth and she struggled to swallow.

"Look," said Aidan, "I didn't call you to get into a debate about the pros and cons of the Restricted Birth Policy versus the Zodiac Trials."

"Why did you call me then?" mumbled Xanthe. "Shouldn't you be spending tonight with *Tabitha?*" Xanthe knew she was being petty and was thankful when Aidan didn't react to the sneer in her voice.

"I'll be seeing her later," he said, "but I was going to ask if you wanted to come for a run. Or, I dunno, we could always get wasted." There was a hint of humour in his voice.

"Tempting," said Xanthe.

"Running or getting wasted? Hey, if we're high, the Capricorn Trial would be a lot more fun."

Xanthe allowed herself to smile. "I might not come from one of the top twelve Zodiac Schools, but that doesn't mean I'm ready to sabotage my chances just yet."

"Fair call," said Aidan. "A run then?"

Xanthe laughed, glancing over at the clock. "A run would be good. Nothing too strenuous, because—"

"Yeah, I know," said Aidan. "Meet you outside Jimmy's in ten."

Xanthe scrawled a quick note for her parents in case they arrived home early, shoved a couple of bites of the sandwich in her mouth, and then headed out of the apartment. Locking the door behind her, she turned to see an old woman hobbling up the stairs.

"Oh," said Meryl pausing a couple of steps from the top, averting her gaze from the tag in Xanthe's ear. "How are you, love?"

Terrified. Angry. Ready to scream. "I'm fine thanks, Meryl. You?"

"Oh, good, good." Meryl gripped the wooden banister with one frail hand. There was an uncomfortable silence where she seemed about to say something more, but didn't.

"All right, well—" Xanthe took a couple of steps down the stairs, squeezing to the side to get past her neighbour.

Meryl's hand shot out and gripped Xanthe's upper arm, her fingers having more strength than Xanthe expected.

"Ouch," said Xanthe, but Meryl's grip didn't loosen. If anything, she squeezed with more ferocity, her grey eyes boring into Xanthe's own.

"Run," she said, her voice low and intense. "Don't fool yourself into thinking that you'll pass the Capricorn Trial. You won't."

"Thanks for the vote of confidence," murmured Xanthe, trying to pull away. The intensity of Meryl's gaze and the grip on her arm held her fixed to the spot.

"I thought Nick and Lisa would pass too," said Meryl, her voice barely above a whisper. "I was so sure of it. They trained so hard."

"Meryl," said Xanthe softly, trying to talk some sense into the old woman, "you know the Trial of '83 was botched. It wasn't just your twins that suffered the consequences of that. *Nobody* passed the Capricorn Trial that year."

Meryl's hand shook as she gazed into the distance. Perhaps she was reliving the footage of an entire cohort of twenty-year-olds dismembered before her eyes.

Xanthe patted the woman's hand with her own, then carefully extricated herself from Meryl's clasp. "I appreciate that you're looking out for me, but the Zodiac Trials are compulsory. Even if I did run, there's nowhere to go—you know that."

Meryl looked down at the worn carpet on the stairs. "Good luck for tomorrow," she at last. "I'd like to tell you that I'll be cheering for you, but . . . I haven't watched in years."

"That's okay," said Xanthe, "I understand." She gave Meryl a little wave and then headed out of the apartment complex and along the street towards Jimmy's. "Crazy old bat," she murmured under her breath.

The sky was dark and drizzly outside the apartment, making it appear later than it really was. The weather was uncharacteristic for December in New South Wales, but it suited her mood. Aidan was waiting for her outside Jimmy's Restaurant. Golden light and easy laughter spilled out of the establishment and onto the footpath.

"Took your time," said Aidan, as Xanthe crossed the road to meet him.

"Sorry. I bumped into my neighbour on the way out. Her kids were part of the Trials of '83."

Aidan scrunched up his nose. People avoided speaking about the embarrassment of the 2083 Capricorn Trial, and yet they all knew about it in grisly detail. It was a rite of passage to watch the banned footage of the trial that—despite its forbidden status—had made its way onto servers all around Australia. One hundred per cent death rate in the very first stage; an entire cohort of twenty years olds wiped out of existence. The UN almost put a stop to Australia's Zodiac Trials there and then. Almost.

"'83 was fucking brutal," said Aidan, as they walked along the footpath. "We won't stand a chance if it's anything like that tomorrow."

Xanthe shrugged. "That was seventeen years ago. Accidents

happen. They fixed the programming on the goats the following year. There hasn't been anything like it since."

"Accidents happen? Yeah, tell that to the parents."

They took off at a slow jog, looping around the gradually darkening park. They made sure to stick to the outer path, keeping a row of trees between them and the small square in the centre of the gardens. Statues representing the twelve signs of the zodiac lined the running circuit, standing like silent martyrs in the lengthening shadows. From within the confines of the leafy park, it was easy to pretend that there weren't dozens of tent cities spreading like cancer along the arteries of Sydney's suburbs just a few blocks away.

"Did you know they used to use *real* goats?" asked Aidan as they drew nearer to the horned statue on the corner with a tail like a fish.

"Really?" asked Xanthe, glancing up at the monstrous figure, slick with rain.

"Only in the first couple of years. They strapped bombs to them, and then whenever a contender got too close . . ."

"Yuck," said Xanthe, jogging past the statue which seemed to be watching her. "That doesn't seem humane."

"Nothing about the Zodiac Trials is humane," said Aidan with a short laugh.

He was right, but there was no point in thinking about it—it was what it was. They all knew there was an overpopulation problem, and the Zodiac Trials were the current solution. There were other benefits, too—bringing revenue into the economy, and tourism as well. Xanthe had heard of people coming all the way from Germany to meet the famous contenders, or to pose on the sites of some of the most brutal massacres.

"Xanthe," said Aidan, guiding her beneath a tree and out of the raindrops. "I'm going ask you something, and I don't want you to flip."

"Okay . . ." said Xanthe, her heart beating uncomfortably fast in her chest. She hugged her arms around herself as the cold threatened to seep through her clothes. "I should have guessed there was some ulterior motive to you wanting to go for a run tonight. What is it?"

Aidan's green eyes looked dark in the shadows beneath the tree. Xanthe wondered if he was going to confess his love to her or something equally as ridiculous. What would she say? Would she deny him again, as she did three years ago? Would she remind him that he was currently dating a blue tag from Aquarius-2? Or would she fall into his arms like some dimwit from a romance novel? Of course, the characters in the novels she read didn't have the threat of the Zodiac Trials tearing them apart like some dystopian version of Romeo and Juliet.

"Have you ever thought of running away?"

His question caught her by surprise. "What?" asked Xanthe, irritation flooding through her veins. "Not you as well."

"Huh?"

Xanthe waved a hand in the air, gesturing in the direction of her apartment. "That's what Meryl was going on about when I bumped into her."

"So?" asked Aidan, moving closer. "Have you?"

Xanthe sighed. "Of course I have," she said, frowning at the guy she'd known for nearly fifteen years.

"And?" prompted Aidan.

"And what?" said Xanthe. "We wouldn't get far, and you know it."

"The Richards' family got to New Zealand," Aidan pointed out. "It was all over the banned media channels. The Kiwi government agreed to give them safe harbour."

"New Zealand has its own overpopulation issues." Xanthe's

tone of voice was sterner than she had meant it to come across. "I'm sorry, but for one family that escapes, how many families are caught? You've seen the news." She pointed in the direction of the square that was shielded by the branches of the tree. "You've seen the bodies."

"We could go by ourselves. It'd be easier with just the two of us rather than a whole family. Better chances. There's a guy who can remove—"

"Don't," said Xanthe. "Just . . . don't."

"But—"

"What about Tabitha?"

Aidan shrugged. "I asked her, of course I asked her. But she's not interested in taking the risk. She has far better chances than either of us at passing the trials when her turn comes."

"Great, so I'm your second choice."

"That's not—"

"Look, we don't have the money or the contacts to pull off something like that. And if we left our parents, your sister, behind—think what would happen to them. Do you really believe they'd be left alone? We just have to go through with the Trials and that's that."

Aidan looked down at the ground, and Xanthe dug her fingernails into the palm of her hand.

"But we'll look after each other, right?" she said, giving him a gentle shove. "We'll help each other through tomorrow's Trial as much as we can. If we get through them all . . ."

She let the thought trail off, distant dreams that weren't worth voicing aloud drifting in the silence between them. A car screeched to a halt on the road nearby, and Xanthe turned towards the sound.

"It's one of those old petrol cars," said Aidan. "God, they were loud. I don't know how people could stand driving them."

There was a burst of laughter as a handful of people fell out of the car doors and onto the road. They were clearly drunk—or high on something—as they leaned heavily against each other and the car took off into the night. Xanthe took a couple of steps closer, drawn to the laughter despite her qualms.

"It's Eliza," said Xanthe as Aidan joined her. "And Rylee, and a couple of others who I don't know. I wonder what they've been up to since school ended."

"Not preparing for the Zodiac Trials, I'd say," said Aidan, and Xanthe nodded in agreement. It wasn't compulsory to study for the Trials, of course, and some teenagers spent the entire two years after school ended partying their lives away. Literally.

Xanthe shook her head as Rylee fell to her knees and vomited on the grass, Eliza unsuccessfully attempting to hold her friend's hair out of harm's way. "Clause 3," murmured Xanthe. "Every member of the population has the right to live a full and rewarding life until the age of twenty."

"Come on," said Aidan, slipping an arm around Xanthe's waist and directing her back onto the running track. "Let's head home—have a decent meal and an early night. I'll see you at the maglev station in the morning."

Xanthe stood under the row of old analogue clocks hanging from the roof of the train station, the weight of her father's embrace still lingering on her skin. He'd held her just a little too long, unable to blink back the tears that revealed his true fear—that this would be the last time he would see his daughter alive. Her mother had been more positive, but even she—usually the stoic one of the couple—had been unable to stop the tears from flowing.

"See you tonight," Xanthe had murmured, cheeks dry, before walking through the security checkpoint on the way into the station.

She glanced up at the clocks counting down to the departure time of 9 a.m. Aidan should have been here by now—the platform was all but empty, the majority of the cohort of red tags already settled on board the maglev train. If he didn't arrive soon . . .

She pushed the thought away. He would make it in time. Only the suicidal—or inebriated—missed the start of the Capricorn Trial.

Last year, the first trial had been held in a national park near Newcastle, and thousands had flocked to Xanthe's home state to get as close to the action as possible. Many more watched the trial in high definition on their wall-screens.

This year, the Capricorn Trial was to be held in Northern Victoria, but with the high-speed magnetic-levitation rail, it meant that Xanthe and all the other contenders from her region could catch the early train and make it to the starting line in plenty of time.

"Red tags, your transport to the Capricorn Trial will be departing in three minutes. Please make your way on board the train."

Xanthe looked around wildly. If Aidan didn't get on this train, if he didn't make it to the start of the trials, then he would—

"Don't look so concerned," said a familiar voice to Xanthe's left.

"Aidan," she said, throwing her arms around him.

"As lovely as this is," said Aidan, extricating himself from her grip, "we really need to board the train."

Xanthe poked him in the ribs, and then followed Aidan along the platform and into the final carriage. It was full of twenty-year-olds in various outfits spilling along the corridor and waving out the windows. Some seemed excited. Others were crying. Those from the elite Zodiac Schools wore their uniforms with pride and Xanthe rolled her eyes. A dead kid was a dead kid regardless of the uniform they wore.

"Good morning," a voice boomed throughout the carriage, "and welcome to the express train direct to this year's Capricorn Trial. This is a high-speed service, so please ensure you remain seated and that your seatbelts are fastened securely."

"You want the window?" asked Aidan, finding an empty seat near the rear of the carriage.

"Sure," said Xanthe, slipping past him and doing up her seatbelt. Aidan swung his backpack off and then collapsed into the chair beside her. It all seemed so normal, like they were going on a nice holiday.

"What'd you bring?" asked Xanthe. The instructions for the trial had been very clear: leave everything at home. Aidan either hadn't read the memo, or he was blatantly ignoring it.

"Here," he said, passing her an earbud from his bag.

"You know they'll take it off you, right? We aren't allowed anything like this and there are no storage facilities."

"I know," he said, shrugging, "but we can listen on the train."

A song from the early twenties pulsed through her earbud. Xanthe groaned. "Not this shit again. Nobody else listens to such ancient music."

"Shush," said Aidan, "and let yourself be cultured."

"What does Tabitha think of your music taste?" Xanthe teased. She didn't mind the music really, it was just so . . . Aidan.

"It's an acquired taste," replied Aidan. "I'm working on developing her appreciation for the classics. We'll get there.

Eventually."

Xanthe laughed. Music from before overpopulation was at the forefront of political thought certainly *was* an acquired taste. They sung about such individualistic concerns as love and sex and drinking. These days, Australian music had far more of a political agenda, and most teenagers didn't bother with it.

"What do you think they sing about in other countries?" Xanthe had asked Aidan one day, when a familiar tune about the excitement of the Zodiac Trials had blasted from the wall-screen.

"They sing about us," Aidan had replied, with a dark expression on his face. Xanthe didn't push for further information. She had begged Aidan plenty of times to stop accessing the banned media channels—she didn't want to see his lifeless body hanging in the centre of the local park.

The train took off silently, pushing Xanthe back in the seat as it sped up, reaching its maximum speed within a few seconds. The landscape zoomed past in a blur of green and brown, and Xanthe closed her eyes, enjoying the feel of Aidan's warm body next to her own, the familiar music wrapping itself protectively around her.

The maglev zoomed across the state border into Victoria without stopping for the usual travel pass inspections, and they had only listened to half the album when the train reached its destination. Aidan stowed the music player in his backpack and shoved it under the seat. "For the ride back," he said, in response to Xanthe's questioning look.

Xanthe bit her lip and nodded silently.

The platform was filled with news reporters and the sky teemed with drones. Xanthe stepped off the train and felt a moment of stardom as people waved at her as though she was someone important. She grasped Aidan's hand so they wouldn't get separated, and then followed the crowd along a narrow dirt path on what appeared to be a farm.

"Terrain looks all right," said Aidan, and Xanthe had to agree. In the past, contenders had to run across canyons, or plough through snow fields, or leap across human-designed landscapes with moving platforms and steep drops. But there was nothing much—from what she could see—that seemed truly difficult. There were hills, and trees, and a few fences, but nothing worth freaking out about.

Xanthe felt marginally better about the day ahead. "Maybe it's the distance that's going to be tough," she said, "or the speed that the goats are set at. Maybe it's not so much about the terrain this time, but about how fast we can run."

"Perhaps," said Aidan.

The first trial tended to be pretty similar every year. Whereas some of the Zodiac Trials were about intellectual capacity or critical thinking, or other traits deemed necessary for Australian citizens, the Capricorn Trial was a test of endurance and athletic ability. It was a race—but they weren't racing against each other.

As she passed a series of cages filled with robotic goats, Xanthe shivered. They weren't racing against each other—they were racing against *them.*

The long row of young adults from the New South Wales maglev train merged with more lines of people from other regions until they swirled together in a large mass. Some sported crimson as though they were proud to be a part of the 2100 cohort. Those from the top Zodiac Schools wore their sports uniforms. Others, like Xanthe, had opted for comfortable, breathable clothing. As she had pulled her clothes on this morning, a nasty little voice had whispered: *These could be the clothes you die in.*

They reached the security zone—a series of beige chutes lined up beside each other in the paddock, barriers guiding the contestants through the maze. Xanthe had seen this before from the comfort of her living room, drone footage explaining the procedures for the contestants.

The line moved quickly, despite the number of contenders. "You," said a woman in black, pointing to Aidan, "over there."

Aidan nodded, walking over to an available chute.

Then the woman turned back to Xanthe. "You, over here. Step in, arms out to the sides."

Xanthe nodded, noting the symbol for the Zodiac Trials embroidered on the woman's shirt—a circle with the twelve zodiac glyphs arranged around the edges, intersected with lines and dots.

Xanthe stepped inside the chute, arms out to the side, waiting for the scanners to confirm that she had no banned items that might give her an unfair advantage in the Trial. There was a beep as her tag was registered, and she relaxed. Soon after the Capricorn Trial began, those with red tags that hadn't attended the trials would be decommissioned—she didn't want a mistake to be made.

"You're good," said a voice from the end of the tunnel, and Xanthe stepped out into the daylight.

Aidan was waiting for her, and he clasped her hand as the crowd surged forward. Xanthe caught a glimpse of a large arena filled with tiered seating and tiny drones hovering overhead, swooping in to get a better look at the contenders.

"Another checkpoint?" asked Xanthe, as they were pushed towards a series of lines. She didn't remember multiple security scans from what she'd seen on the wall-screen, but perhaps they weren't shown everything because it would make boring viewing.

Aidan shook his head, his height allowing him to see what was happening at the front of the line they joined. "No," he said, as the line moved forward. "Looks like they've changed the rules."

Xanthe frowned, telling herself that it was okay—that all of the 2100 cohort were in the same situation, that they were all just as confused. As they reached the front of their line, a man representing the Zodiac Trials was holding what looked like a large zip tie. Xanthe raised an eyebrow.

"Hands behind your back," he said in a bored tone, and Xanthe realised what he going to do.

"No," she said, shaking her head.

Aidan lay a hand on her shoulder. "Come on," he said quietly, "it'll be okay. Look, everyone's getting it."

Xanthe's heart raced as she looked across to the left, where other contenders appeared just as confused and panicky as her. But here and there along the line were those in the uniform of the Zodiac Schools, looking calm and smug.

As the man secured her hands firmly behind her, the tie cut painfully into her wrists. Xanthe took a deep breath and gazed ahead towards the starting line. The beginning point of the Capricorn Trial was marked with a crimson banner, high in the air. There was one lower down as well, at waist height, and already people were lining up along it. But their heads . . .

"What's going—" Xanthe began, and then the man slipped something white over her head, blocking out her view. A strap was pulled tight around her forehead, and another around her throat.

"It's too tight," said Xanthe, but already the man was pushing her forward so that she stumbled towards the crowd of people that she could hear, but no longer see. The material of the blindfold was light, but it completely obscured her vision, and it covered her whole face, making it feel like she couldn't breathe. "Aidan," she cried out, turning back towards her friend.

"Move along," said a voice, giving her a rough shove so that she almost fell over. She desperately wanted to put her hands out in front of her to keep from bumping into anyone, but the cord around her wrists was impossible to move, digging painfully into her skin.

Xanthe walked slowly forward, listening intently for Aidan's voice calling out her name, forcing herself to breathe slowly, not to panic. In all of her nightmares about the Capricorn Trial, she had never imagined that she would be separated from her best friend before it had even begun. Or that she would be blindfolded, with her hands tied behind her.

"Welcome to the Zodiac Trials," boomed Greyson's voice and Xanthe jumped. The audience somewhere high above her erupted into cheers and Xanthe started to panic.

"Aidan!" she cried out, turning around. But she felt disorientated, wondering if she was even facing the right direction. "Aidan!"

The noise from the crowd completely drowned out her voice. It seemed impossible that Aidan would find her now, and she bit her lip hard to stop from crying. Crying wouldn't help anyone here at the Capricorn Trial. Xanthe had a sudden vision of her parents at home, hands clasped together, red eyes peering intently at the wall-screen. Then she thought of Meryl, wall-screen silent, gazing at the photos of her twins hanging on the wall.

"This Trial will run the same as past Capricorn Trials—a game of cat and mouse. Except, of course, that it's a game of human and goat." Greyson's laugh echoed around the tiered seating, sending chills up Xanthe's arms. "And this time, it's *blind* human and goat."

Xanthe took a couple of steps forward and felt movement around her—she had reached the crowd gathered at the starting line. The blindfold reminded her uncomfortably of the bags placed over the heads of those hung for their crimes in the town square so bystanders didn't see their eyeballs popping out.

There was pressure behind her as more people from the 2100 cohort joined the starting line, and she was crushed against the person in front. Xanthe breathed slowly through her nose, trying to calm herself.

"The contenders will have a ten-minute head start on the goats. This will be a test of athleticism, endurance, and also critical thinking—is it best to take the most direct route across the fields, or to leave the crowd and skirt around to the finish line?"

Xanthe wondered how on earth she was even going to find the finish line. It was uncomfortably warm, pinned against the other contenders, and the buzz of electricity in the air clawed its way down her throat.

"And, as always, the goats will explode when they come within a metre's range of a competitor."

"Xanthe."

The voice came from somewhere to her left, and Xanthe tried to move towards it, pushing people out of the way with her shoulders, but the crowd was jammed too tight.

"Move," she said, pushing harder, and then the people beside her jostled around and she was free.

"Aidan?"

"Here."

She turned towards his voice and then she was beside him, laying her head against his chest.

"It's going to be okay," he whispered. "This might actually work to our advantage."

Xanthe didn't see how he figured that, but Greyson's voice was booming over the crowd again, and there was no chance to ask.

"It is a privilege to become a citizen of Australia, and only

94

the best deserve this right. However, in the past, 'the best' actually meant 'the wealthy.' The Restricted Birth Policy was a mark of shame in Australia's history, and I apologise unreservedly to those impacted by our previous government's narrow-minded decisions. The Zodiac Trials are a much fairer way to decide who gets to continue our society."

Xanthe took a deep breath, and it was her and Aidan standing alone under a tree, and he was asking her to run away with him.

"So, without further ado, let's get this Trial underway." The signature music of the Zodiac Trials surged out of speakers around the area. Greyson didn't wait longer than a heartbeat before he said: "Ready, and . . . Go!"

The competitors surged forward and Xanthe had no choice but to move with them. She trusted that Aidan was being pushed along in the same direction. All she could think about was not falling over and being trampled.

On the inside of the blindfold, a dimly glowing beacon appeared.

"A map," she said excitedly, as she felt the runners started to spread out. "Aidan, there's a map."

"Not quite," said a voice beside her. "Come on, keep talking so we can stick together."

He was right—the glowing beacon wasn't quite as useful as a map. It simply highlighted the finish line, with an arrow indicating the direction and distance—9986 metres.

"Ten ks," she said falling into a jog beside Aidan, wishing that she could put her hands out in front of her. "That's not so bad."

Xanthe stumbled over uneven ground and nearly fell, so she slowed her pace a fraction. A twisted ankle would spell disaster in this trial.

A cry to her left made her pause. "Wait," she said, and then another contender barrelled into her, pushing her arm into something sharp.

"Ouch," she cried, as she slammed into what felt like a barbed-wire fence.

"Sorry," they mumbled, pulling away.

Xanthe stepped away from the wire, feeling warm rivulets running down her skin where the barbs had punctured her arm. Bending down, she felt with her leg and shoulder for the wires. It was more difficult than she imagined it would be, and she cursed the lost time as she finally slipped through the fence.

"What's our strategy?" she asked Aidan as they started to jog again, listening carefully for any more cries of pain.

"Same as we agreed upon," said Aidan, "there's no point in changing, just because we're blindfolded."

"Okay," said Xanthe. "Let's go."

As the ground began to ascend, she swerved to the left, away from the main stream of runners she could hear all around her, panting with exertion. "This way," she said quietly, running as fast as she dared, hoping she wasn't going to run into a fence, or a tree, or fall off a cliff.

The ground veered sharply upwards and she stumbled several times, falling painfully against rocks, but always climbing upwards, putting distance between them and the majority of the contenders. The air grew colder and the ground was littered with rocks, but this gave her hope that the goats wouldn't bother coming this way. Previous tapes of the Capricorn Trials showed that the majority would follow the main flow of competitors, and only a small percentage would veer from this dominating heat signature. Xanthe hoped that she would be safely at the finish line by the time the goats were looking further afield.

The low *hoot* of the horn announcing that the goats had

been released was louder than Xanthe imagined it would be from her viewing of past trials. The sound was like a rumble of thunder combined with the toot from an old steam train.

"Run, run, run," said Aidan, from her left, and Xanthe increased her speed, following the curve of the mountain upwards. The glowing digits on the inside of the blindfold showed that they'd barely travelled a kilometre over the past ten minutes. She hoped that they'd reach flat land soon so they could make better time, and that their plan wouldn't backfire. If it did . . .

"I think we're at the top," murmured Aidan, and Xanthe took a moment to rest, sucking deep breaths of cool air into her lungs through the bag over her head. She could hear shouts and footsteps from somewhere below, but up here on the ridge, they seemed to be the only people on earth. A buzzing sound to Xanthe's right shattered the illusion.

"Drones," said Aidan, "broadcasting our journey to living rooms all around the globe. Wave hello to your mother. Oh wait, we can't."

Xanthe ignored him, her sweat turning cold. She ran a few steps further along the ridge and watched the distance counter on the inside of her blindfold reduce to eight kilometres. Eight kilometres of unknown terrain that they would have to traverse blindfolded. The thought terrified her.

"Let's follow this ridge," suggested Xanthe, "if that's what it is. It seems to be heading in the right direction and hopefully it'll keep us above the goats until we are nearer to the finish line."

"Okay."

Aidan fell into step behind her and Xanthe hurried along as fast as she dared, wishing there was more of a breeze so that she could hear the sway of tree branches rather than being fearful of running into a trunk at any moment.

After a few minutes of stumbling over rocks and jarring her knees when she tripped over uneven bits of ground, a strange sound echoing up from the canyon below made her pause.

"Do you hear that?" she whispered, as the faint beeping drifted up the hill.

Aidan stopped beside her, panting heavily from fear or exertion. "Yeah, I hear it. It seems to be getting louder."

Beep. Beep. Beep. There was a pregnant pause and a moment later an explosion, coupled with screams of terror. "Run!" came a faint voice from below.

"It's the goats," said Aidan. "They make noise this year. I suppose because we can't see them they thought it'd be fairer for us if we could hear them."

"Fairer, right. Come on," said Xanthe, as several more explosions, followed by screams, filled the air. None of the beeps were coming from up on the ridge, so Xanthe was pleased with their decision to climb. They made good speed now that the ground was flatter, and Xanthe increased her pace, despite her regular stumbles over logs and around trees.

A series of scrabbling sounds came from their right. "Hello?" called a voice.

Xanthe stayed silent, jogging past the contender climbing up the hill.

"Hello," said Aidan, and Xanthe rolled her eyes. The Capricorn Trial was not about working together, it was better for them to put as much distance as they could between themselves and the others.

"I'm Maria. Can you help me?" asked the voice. "If we work together, maybe you can get my blindfold off."

"No," said Xanthe, stopping and turning back. "We can't help you."

"Aww, Xanthe," said Aidan. "It's a good idea. If we can see, we'll move a lot faster."

"No," Xanthe repeated. "They wouldn't have given us blindfolds just to be okay with us taking them off."

"I'll be quick," said Maria.

Xanthe turned away, continuing along the ridge, but Aidan must have helped the girl, because a moment later she was *whooping* and running quickly past.

"Thank y—"

The whine of a drone cut off the girl's voice, and the next rock that Xanthe stumbled over felt wet and soft and warm.

Aidan was silent as they continued their journey, but more and more contenders were joining them on the ridge now. Every time she heard the scrabbling sounds, Xanthe listened for the tell-tale beep of a goat.

Xanthe put her head down, running faster so that she could pass them rather than be left at the back of the crowd. "Woah," said Xanthe as the ground dropped away beneath her and she fell hard against a rock, rolling over twice before coming to a halt, blood filling her mouth as all air was knocked out of her lungs.

"Xanthe?" came Aidan's concerned voice. "Xanthe answer me, are you okay?"

Xanthe tried to answer, but her voice came out as a squeak.

"Don't touch me," said someone else.

"Sorry," said Aidan. "Just looking for a friend."

"Here," said Xanthe, her voice barely above a whisper. "Aidan."

A foot reached out and brushed her own, and a moment later Aidan was kneeling on the ground next to her. "Oh thank god, I thought you might have fallen down the cliff."

"Nah, just winded." Xanthe sat up, pushing against the ground with her tied hands. Aidan leant against her, chest heaving with exertion. Around them, the sound of running feet filled their ears. And then the sound of a distant, but clearly audible *beep.* The sound filled Xanthe with dread.

"Hurry," said Aidan, stumbling to his feet. "We've only got four kilometres to go, and it seems to be going downhill."

Xanthe and Aidan half-ran, half slid down the cliff face. The occasional scream and thwack told Xanthe that someone had either fallen off the edge or run into a tree. The term 'breakneck speed' suddenly held new meaning.

As fast as they ran, the beeping seemed to be getting louder, and there were multiple beeps now—half a dozen of the metal goats on their trail. Every now and then there would be a pause in the beeps and an explosion as one of the goats caught up with the tail of the procession fleeing down the mountain.

The ground levelled out abruptly, and Xanthe took off at a sprint.

"One . . . kilometre . . ." breathed Aidan, but Xanthe was too exhausted to reply. She put her head down and ran as fast as she could, watching as the glowing digits on the inside of the mask counted down. Six hundred metres. Five hundred and fifty. Five hundred.

Thud.

Xanthe fell to the ground, dazed, her head erupting into a ball of pain. The ground seemed to convulse beneath her, and she lay back on the grass, groaning. "Aidan," she said blearily, reaching out with her leg. She found the rough bark of the trunk that she had run into. "Aidan," she said again, rolling over and feeling in the other direction. She found his body next to another tree, barely a metre away.

She nudged him with her foot. *Beep, beep, beep.* Head screaming with pain, Xanthe sat up, swivelling so that her back was facing Aidan. Reaching her hands out behind her, she gripped his hand. Hot tears leaked out of the sides of her eyes as the high-pitched beep drew impossibly close. This was it, it was all over. But at least they were together.

"Xanthe?" murmured Aidan.

"I'm here," said Xanthe, squeezing tightly.

Beep, beep, beep.

There was a pause in the beeping and Xanthe closed her eyes, knowing what was coming next.

Aidan stirred, pushing her hands away. Was he going to try to keep running? It was no use, the goat was too close. Then he flipped around to cover Xanthe with his body as a loud bang made her jump, and all noise reduced to a single muffled whine.

Aidan's body spasmed once and then lay still, something wet soaking through his blindfold and dripping onto Xanthe. With some effort, she rolled him to the side, her ears ringing from the explosion. Turning her back to Aidan, her hands moved gently across her best friend's back, feeling shards of metal piercing his skin.

"No, no, no," she sobbed, but all she could hear was the ringing in her ears and a strange buzz. Recognising the sound, she wished her hands weren't tied behind her back so that she could give the drone the finger.

Aidan was dead. Even if the shards hadn't pierced a vital organ, the poison covering the metal would have done the trick. And she would be joining him soon if she didn't move. Five hundred metres left. Five hundred metres to live.

Staggering to her feet, Xanthe took off towards the finish line. As she ran, consumed by the darkness of the blindfold, visions of Aidan filled her mind. Aidan at school, passing her notes. Aidan asking her out—and Xanthe saying no. Aidan asking her if she'd thought of running away. Together.

The tears flowed freely down her cheeks now, soaking into the material of the blindfold.

Four hundred metres. Three hundred metres.

If there were any goats coming up behind her, she couldn't

tell—the sounds around her were muffled and warped.

Two hundred metres. One hundred metres.

If she was able to hear, surely there would be the sound of the crowd cheering her on.

Fifty metres. Twenty.

Xanthe crossed the finish line and collapsed on the ground, sobbing. The glowing digits on the inside of the blindfold shifted to say: 'Congratulations! You have passed the Capricorn Trial.' But it was slim comfort when her best friend lay broken on the unforgiving farmland.

Somebody removed her blindfold and the sunlight was harsh in her eyes—surely it should be grey and miserable, not blue cloudless skies.

"Congratulations," said one of the crew, helping her to her feet and snipping off the zip tie. "There'll be a bit of a ceremony once the field has cleared. For now, head over to first aid."

Xanthe glanced down at her blood-soaked shirt, not having the strength to tell the worker that most of the blood wasn't hers.

The air of excitement during the ceremony made Xanthe feel sick. The top ten contenders were awarded with trophies, shaped like the statue in the park back home—a horned goat with a fish tail. Everyone else was presented with a copper medal hung from a crimson cord. Xanthe accepted her medal with little fanfare, shoved it into her pocket and turned to board the waiting train.

The number of people boarding the maglev back to Sydney was less than half of what it had been in the morning. Despite the greater choice in seats, Xanthe walked along to the final carriage.

Taking the same seat as in the morning, she rummaged around until she found Aidan's bag. Pulling out the music player, she placed the buds in her ears and clicked play on the album from the 2020s that they had been listening to just a few hours ago. Just a few hours. It felt like a lifetime.

There were other things in the bag, too—a jumper, a water bottle, and a diary that she didn't dare to open. Shaking slightly, Xanthe pulled the large jumper on and snuggled down in the seat, hugging her arms around herself.

She'd done it. She'd passed the Capricorn Trial. She tried to ignore the fact that in exactly one month's time, she would be summoned to the next trial—Aquarius. And she wouldn't have someone like Aidan to save her this time.

About the Author:

Alanah Andrews is a Kiwi / Australian dystopian and science fiction writer. You can download a copy of her YA dystopian novella The Harvest *from her website: www.alanahandrews.com*

THE JUDAS GOAT

Stephen Herczeg

Simon's eyes flickered open. He was lying on a hard, dirt floor. A few strands of straw lay scattered around him. They came from the bedding of the nearby cot.

This room was certainly very alien to Simon's mind.

He sat up, his head still groggy.

Was I drugged? By whom?

He peered around.

He was in a small cell, enclosed by rough-cut, brick walls. A thick wooden door with a small window represented the only way in or out. High up in the centre of the nearest wall was a tiny, barred window. The window was the size of a single brick; thick wooden bars prevented any thought of exit. The only light came from tiny gaps at the top of the wall opposite the door where the sheet metal ceiling met the brick wall.

He felt his head. Closed his eyes for a moment. Tried to retrace his last thoughts.

Images came to his mind. His lover, Helena. His brother, Thomas. All three of them in the makeshift shack that Simon lived in. Then darkness.

He stood and paced the room, investigating each corner. It was possibly a prison cell. The bed was functional but looked uncomfortable. A hole in the floor in one corner was for servicing his ablutions. Through the small window, he could see the ceiling of another room. Simon dragged the cot across and stood on its edge to reach the window. With his head brushing the ceiling of his cell, he could barely manage to view the opposite wall of the neighbouring cell.

Frustrated, he jumped down and dragged the cot back into position.

Through the tiny window in the door, the first couple of feet of a small, dark passageway was visible. No light shone further down to indicate how far the passage extended.

He flopped down on the bed and tried to work out where he was and how he'd ended up there.

He thought long and hard.

Have I been arrested?

He couldn't remember breaking any of the strict laws of the city. The governing prefecture were incredibly controlling when it came to the law. Any indiscretion was met with almost violent intervention.

Such was the way in the lands of B'droo. They could trace the history of the city back to the years after the fall. The legends abound about the great cataclysm that rained down from the sky. The seas boiled and threw up clouds that covered the lands for decades, blocking out the sun and bringing famine and destruction.

B'droo had been a small community in a remote valley in the hills to the south-west of the largest metropolis of the country. Refugees from the coast had moved inland as the seas rose and swamped their cities and coastal towns. Many had flocked to the isolated village and it had grown to a mighty city within a decade.

For many ages they had lived a relatively peaceful existence, nestled in the mountain valley, secure from the neighbouring communities by virtue of their remoteness and difficulty in access. The narrow mountain passes that were the only avenues to the city were guarded by their militia and by nature itself.

It was, in fact, rare that the city received visitors and the populace was forbidden to leave unless accompanied by a military escort or under a prefectural mandate.

Simon's brother, Thomas, had been granted such a mandate. He belonged to one of the scavenger teams that embarked on long journeys beyond the valley. Their task was to search the ancient abandoned ruins and return with any items that could be useful to the community.

Simon was a teacher. He was far removed from any notion of leaving the city. He was a model civilian, not even risking the ire of the leaders by questioning their philosophies. Some of his supervisors deemed him to be ineffective as an individual mind, but a source of joy as a simple adherent to procedures and protocols.

He could think of nothing he had done to end up in a jail cell such as this.

Simon looked up and stared at the wall across from him.

The brick? It's not used much in the city. Only the prison, the town hall and the house of Justice used that type of brick. It could even be a basement room in the school. Maybe this was all some elaborate prank by the students.

He dismissed that thought. His students were far too young to undertake such a trick.

He got to his feet and went to the door. Pushing his mouth as far through the tiny window as he could he yelled into the gloom. "Hey, where am I? Why am I here?"

His pleas were met with a cloying silence as the last echoes faded.

He flopped back on the cot in frustration and dropped his head into his hands.

A thin voice floated out from the thick stone walls. "Simon?"

He recognised the voice immediately. "Helena?" he replied, "Where are you?"

"I'm in a brick cell. I don't know how I got here."

Simon edged up to the interior window. "I think you're next to me. Talk louder."

"How can I get out of here?" she asked, her voice shrill.

Simon grabbed the cot again and dragged it to the opposite wall. He stood on the side, and precariously balanced, directed his voice to the little window. "Look up," he said, "there's a small window." He reached up and thrust his fingers through the tiny gap in the bars. "Can you see my fingers?" he asked.

Within moments, Helena's fingers entwined with his own. "It is you. I can't believe it. How did we get here?"

"I have no idea. All I can remember is being at home. There's you and . . ." He hesitated for a moment, searching his memories. ". . . And Thomas."

"Thomas? Does he have something to do with this?" she asked.

His mood darkened when the vision of his brother came to mind. "I don't know, but I've got a bad feeling about this."

"But you two are so close, why would he do this to you?"

"He—"

"There's someone at the door."

Simon moved to his door and peered through the window. He assumed there was a corridor running in front of the doors, but there was nothing he could see.

Helena's voice filtered through from the next cell. "Who's there? Thomas? Is that you?"

There was a noise of flesh slapping on flesh, a yelp, then silence.

Simon returned to the cot and climbed up in a desperate attempt to look into Helena's cell. He pressed his cheek to the ceiling and strained to see anything through the tiny window. "Helena? Helena? What's happening?"

He was greeted with silence.

"Helena?" His cries grew more pitiful as the silence consumed every one of them. Finally he slunk down from his perch, turned over the cot and collapsed onto it.

"What is happening?" he asked into the silent void around him.

He was surrounded by four walls made of brick, metal and wood, with a dirt floor. Very basic and consisting of only a single metal door and a small barred window at eye height in the wall next to him. Light filtered in through the small gaps running around the join between walls and ceiling.

Thomas sat and stared at the door. He had peered through the window and been met with another solid wall exactly like the one behind him. The adjacent cell was empty. He'd yelled into it without response multiple times.

He looked at his clothing. Gone were his jeans and t-shirt. Favourites of his that he had found in an abandoned warehouse a few years back. He was wearing a simple homespun smock, barely a tunic. His feet were bare, and gone were his leather boots. His hands were also bare of the golden rings he wore, souvenirs of his many journeys out of B'droo.

The last thing Thomas could remember was standing before Simon and Helena in the main room of Simon's shack. Some friends had just left and Thomas, as always, was the last to leave. They'd all partaken in one last drink from Simon's own special stash, then he had woken up here.

Had he been knocked unconscious, robbed and dragged to this god-forsaken place?

And where was he anyway?

He tried to picture all the buildings of B'droo. The style was notable of the *newer* structures. Original buildings tended to be of one material, all brick, all wood, but newer buildings were built from assorted material, usually anything that could be salvaged or scavenged from the surrounding areas.

He knew this wasn't the Jail, the Hall of Justice, or even the Prefect's house. They were all original structures and mostly made of brick.

The fact that light was coming in from the small holes at the top of one of the walls, indicated that he was on the outer wall and above ground.

He thought of the locations. In his mind, none of them had the layout that he'd seen here.

Thomas moved over to what he thought must be the external wall. He examined it closer. Pressed at the bricks, the metal, the wood. Nothing moved. He thumped a fist on the wood and metal parts, eliciting some dull thuds but not much more.

Defeated, he trudged back to his cot and slumped down against the wall.

His eyes began to close as sleep claimed him. Through his dream-state he heard his name being called. Over and over again. The voice sounded familiar. Very familiar.

"Thomas."

His eyes snapped open and he heard his name again with a hint of urgency.

"Thomas."

He stood up and turned.

Framed in the small window was Helena. His mind's eye

kicked into overdrive. Her face appeared in his thoughts, as it always had, her beautiful, clear complexion, her dazzling blue eyes, a radiant sun providing a corona around her luxuriant hair.

He blinked and focused back on the real image.

Helena's face was far from radiant. Her hair was matted with dirt. Her face smeared with the same and peppered with several bruises and welts.

He rushed to the window.

"What happened? You're hurt. Who did this?" he blurted out.

Tears formed at the corners of Helena's eyes and made clean tracks through the grime as they slid down her cheeks.

She bowed her head in shame. "Simon. I don't know why, but he's lost his mind."

"What? Where are we?"

"I don't know. I've seen other rooms. They are the same as these. I don't think we are in B'droo anymore."

"He's sold us as slaves."

"No, I don't think that's his plan."

"Why? Why would he do this?"

Helena looked up at Thomas' strong face, a sliver of light in her eyes. "He's always been jealous of you. Even before me. You are older. You are stronger. You had more of your parents' respect. And then I came along and spoiled everything. He thinks we're sleeping together," she said.

"That idiot. I . . . I admit I've had feelings for you, but you fell for my brother. End of story. Why would he think I'd betray his trust like this?"

"He's weak," Helena said, "I see that now. He's not a real man. He can only prey on the weak. Like me."

"What do you mean?"

Helena turned her face up to reveal the extent of her

bruising.

Thomas' eyes opened wide in shock. "He did this to you?"

She nodded her head slowly, then dropped her chin in shame. "Last night, just after we were brought here. He came for me. Dragged me away. Beat me up. Had his way with me."

Helena burst into tears.

Thomas reached through the bars and traced a finger along Helena's jawline.

"It will be fine. I'll get us out of here. Then I'll put a stop to Simon's plans," he said, a defiant but slightly defeated tone in his voice.

She looked deep into his eyes, the first vestiges of love shining through her misery.

Suddenly, the door to Helena's cell flung inward.

"Move away from the window," a commanding voice shouted.

Thomas caught sight of a man dressed in combat fatigues and a crash helmet before something thudded into his outstretched hand. He snatched it back and cradled it to ease the pain.

A hatch on the little window slammed shut.

Thomas pushed at it with his good hand, but it wouldn't budge. He heard Helena's squeals as she was dragged from the cell.

"Helena, Helena, Helena," he shouted.

There was nothing but silence.

Simon lay awake in the dark cell. Questions pounded his brain. Where was Helena? Where was that bastard Thomas? What he done with Helena?

The door in the cell next to him slammed open, jolting him awake. He listened as something was dragged in and dumped on the floor. Footsteps led away, and the door was slammed shut and locked.

"Helena?" he whispered, his heart in his throat.

Nothing. Almost silence with a laboured breath running on the edge of his hearing limits.

"Helena?" he said louder.

Finally, the rustle of the dirt told him that someone stirred.

"Helena?" he yelled.

A voice replied groggily. "What? Hello? Who?" said the voice.

The voice went silent for a moment, the owner composing themselves before letting out a groan.

"Helena are you alright? What has that bastard done to you?"

No one answered, only the sound of a woman crying floated into Simon's cell through the tiny window.

"Helena? What happened?" he shouted, "Tell me."

"I'm sorry. I just," she started then groaned in pain.

Simon stood up and dragged his cot across to the opposite wall. He tipped it on its side and straddled it to gain access to the window.

He thrust his fingers through the bars of the little window and groped at the air inside Helena's cell.

"I'm here," he said as he wiggled his fingers.

Within moments he felt the warm touch of another human being.

"Simon, I'm so sorry. I thought I could talk sense into him, but he just beat me and then . . ." She stopped mid-sentence and pulled her fingers away.

"What did he do?" shouted Simon, repeating the phrase louder with each reiteration until he was almost screaming.

"His hands. All over me. It's what he's wanted for so long. I should never have trusted him."

"I'll kill him for this."

"How? We won't leave this place alive. He wants us both dead. He just wants to prolong the agony. He's sick. I'm sure of it. Especially after today."

Simon's face turned red with rage. His voice began to slur as the fury built inside him. "I'm gonna . . . I'll . . . When I see him, I will . . ."

Unseen by Simon, a tube extended from a tiny hole in the wall beneath the window. Helena pressed a small rubber bulb and a colourless gas escaped.

Simon, still raging about his brother, took a deep breath to fill his lungs and breathed the gas in. His eyes swam, and he fell from his perch, slumping to the ground in a heap.

"Thank God for that," Helena muttered.

"Thomas?"

His name smashed through the gloom in his mind. He opened his eyes and was met with darkness.

"Thomas?"

This time the voice was more urgent. He looked across and saw a figure outlined in the small window. Finally, recognition dawned.

"Helena?" Thomas said, as he sat bolt upright. He leapt off the cot and moved to the window. "Helena? It *is* you, isn't it?"

The figure nodded. "Yes. Simon brought me back to this damn cell after he'd finished with me."

"Finished with you?"

"Yes, he questioned me about our *relationship*. I kept telling him there was no relationship. That it was all in his mind. He backhanded me so hard I fell to the floor."

"That bastard."

"Then he picked me up and beat me again. I kept telling

him that there was nothing. That he'd imagined it. He's gone crazy with jealousy. He just kept blaming you. Saying he was going to kill you. I tried to convince him you were innocent, but he beat me further. Everything hurts, I just want to die."

She burst into tears.

Thomas reached through the bars and caressed her cheek. Helena pulled away with a slight squeal of pain. "This is ridiculous, we need to get out of here now."

He walked to the door and banged on it with all his might and yelled into the darkness. "Let us out of here, you crazy asshole."

A figure appeared on the other side of the door. Thomas stepped back in shock, then raced back to the door to try and see their face. The person was wearing a face mask and helmet.

"Who the hell are you?"

The figure simply held up a plastic tube before the tiny window. A puff of invisible gas poured out and enveloped Thomas' stunned face.

He sniffed and sucked a lung full of the noxious odour. The effect was immediate, and he collapsed to the dirt floor.

"I am very impressed," said the man who called himself the Ringmaster. He was well into his fifties, a remarkable accomplishment in this day and age. His silvering hair was brushed back in a neat and short style. He wore a fading, but elegant formal shirt with a red vest over the top, highlighted by a red cravat around his neck. His pencil thin moustache and triangular goatee gave him the look of the devil.

Helena knew this man was one step away from the devil and planned to play her hand carefully.

The Ringmaster smiled and continued. "You have delivered two brothers—once loving siblings who would do anything to protect each other. But add a little bit of sex and subversion into the equation and they are almost ready to kill each other," he said, smiling.

The Ringmaster looked out of his office at the arena below—a large circular ring with a sand floor and high walls made of all manner of detritus. Row upon row of seats ringed the arena—enough to sit two thousand people.

"Tomorrow night will be the highlight of the festival of Capricornia. At this time of year, mid-summer, the temperatures soar, and the people become distracted. They need their blood games, or they become bored and their minds turn to things such as how horrible their pathetic little lives really are. We can't have any uprisings—that would cost too much in the way of policing. Instead—" he waved an arm at the arena—"We have the games. The little people can come and watch blood spilled for several hours then return to their little lives."

He leaned forward and rested his chin on steepled fingers. "That's why we utilise people like you. Those willing to corrupt the innocent and lead them to slaughter," he said.

"I only have one goal. To help my people. You offered a large reward, I accepted and delivered. That's all," replied Helena.

The Ringmaster leaned back and reached into the top drawer of the ancient oaken desk. He tossed a small leather pouch across the table.

Helena picked it up and spilled the contents into her hand. Several precious gems sparkled on her palm. She smiled to herself. She had never seen such wealth.

"The down payment. Enough to keep the slum pit that you call home alive for at least another five years. If your boys put on a decent show, then you will receive even greater rewards." He smiled. "If they do a great job then I might consider bringing you into my employ. We can always use another Judas Goat that can bring such virtuous specimens to us in the name of entertainment."

The girl poured the gemstones back into the pouch and looked up at the Ringmaster. She smiled and said, "I spent a year of my life working on those two men. Part of my heart is with them, but not much. When I took on your assignment all I thought of was the safety of my parents and my town. Let me go home and distribute this wealth." She held up the pouch. "If this is the size of the reward, then I will have to think very seriously about your offer. After all, a girl needs the finer things life can provide, don't you think?" she said.

The Ringmaster laughed. "I think we may have a long and prosperous future together, Miss Helena."

The Ringmaster stood on a small podium suspended high above the dirt floored arena below. He turned to the crowd that was threatening to overflow the rows of seats before him.

"Friends, visitors, residents . . . I bid you welcome, on this mid-summer's evening, to the blood games of Capricornia."

The crowd erupted with excitement.

"This is a tradition that has been held at this time every year, in this wonderous city of N'wra since the fall." He turned around to face the audience on the opposite side. "Tonight, we have something a little special to begin proceedings with. Two brothers. When they were discovered their bond was unbreakable, a bond like all true siblings hold. Our honoured guest introduced herself into the mix and bred discontent between the brothers. Tonight, we will see if the fruit of that work comes to bear."

He held out a hand towards Helena, seated in the front row of the opposite stand. She stood, her long red gown flowing down her legs to the ground, and waved to the crowd.

"Firstly, let us thank the provider of our entertainment."

The crowd clapped and cheered Helena. She blew several kisses to members of the crowd then took her seat.

"Let the games begin," shouted the Ringmaster and made his way from the podium across to his seat next to Helena.

He leaned in and spoke to her. "I do hope this is half as entertaining as I have been promoting or there could be blood. The wrong blood."

Helena swallowed on a dry throat. She was certain that she had baited the two men to the point of bloodshed. Regardless, she spied the exits in case things went south.

Simon woke. He blinked his eyes to clear the rime and looked around his cell. A dim, yellow light filtered in through the gaps between ceiling and wall. He was on the floor, next to his overturned cot. He sat up and held his head for a moment to nullify the grogginess.

It was then he saw his cell door was ajar.

He approached the opening and peered through. The corridor outside was in gloom.

Simon walked down the corridor, running one hand along the wall, searching for any deviation in the surface that might be an exit.

The floor rose in a gentle slope as he moved along. He heard something. It sounded like ocean waves crashing on a shore. He carried on until the floor rose sharply and became a set of earthen stairs leading up.

Simon peered upwards. Above, there was only gloom. He peered back down the corridor. There was only darkness that way as well, and the thought of returning to his depressing cell spurred him on.

He looked up the staircase. He feared the unknown but decided that whatever waited at the top of the stairs was less frightening than the alternative.

At the top of the staircase he found another short corridor. At the end was a bright outline of a doorway.

His spirits soared. He'd found the way out.

His only hope now was to find Helena and get out of this place. Wherever this place was.

Thomas sat up and spat out the dirt that crusted his lips. He'd spent the night with his face plastered to the floor by the drool seeping from his mouth.

Wiping the rest of the grime away with the back of his hand, he noticed the door of his cell was ajar.

He rose to his feet and stepped through the entrance. The corridor beyond was dark and only as wide as his cell.

He kept one hand on the wall and made his way along the corridor as fast as he could manage without tripping.

A noise filtered through into the passage. It sounded like a crowd of people cheering.

Weird. Maybe it's waves or trees. There can't be that many people here.

As Thomas continued on, the noise grew louder, then ceased altogether.

His journey was interrupted by an almost perpendicular wall that reared up out of the gloom. Luckily, his outstretched hand found it first, rather than his face. He found a set of crude steps carved into the wall and began to ascend.

At the top, he found another long passageway with a door outlined by bright light at the end.

Helena's through that door, I know it. If not, then hopefully it's Simon.

He raced towards the doorway.

Simon opened the door, blinding himself with the light. He staggered across the threshold, allowing his light-starved eyes time to adjust.

The ground was soft underfoot, and he saw that he stood on yellow sand that stretched out across a wide open, circular space. A wall made of metal objects fused together enclosed the entire area. It only rose up a few metres, but he wasn't sure he could climb over it. A line of flaming torches ringed the entire circle. They threw light down towards him and smoke above, obscuring his view of what lay beyond the wall.

The sound intruded his thoughts again, much louder. It was a crowd. Cheering. He was right. He peered through the smoke, trying to see them.

Nothing.

He searched around and found several racks of weapons lining the nearby walls. *It's a gladiator pit. Oh, God. I'm a teacher, not a fighter.* The racks held long makeshift spears, short swords that were more like machetes, knives and shields.

I need to survive, I need to find Helena. He examined the weapons. First, he chose a large shield but could barely lift it. He switched to a smaller shield and reached for a long, wickedly sharp spear. *Shield for protection. Spear for distance.*

Simon moved around the arena, searching for a way out and peering up through the smoke to catch a glimpse of the audience above. He managed to view vague faces through the smoke but couldn't recognise anyone. *This is definitely not B'droo.*

Without warning a primal cry erupted from across the arena. Simon turned his head and saw a figure standing in a doorway opposite.

Thomas?

The figure picked up a short sword. He turned back and glared at Simon. "You bastard," Thomas screamed and ran towards his brother.

"Thomas? What? I—" Simon stuttered before Thomas was on him. He dragged his shield up just as his older brother brought his sword down with an overhead swing. Thomas rained blows down on the shield which began to buckle under the onslaught and drove Simon to one knee.

Simon managed to swing his spear around and caught Thomas in the side with the point. Thomas fell sideways as the pain overcame his fury.

He dropped to his knees and put a hand to the wound. The blood sparked another spate of seething rage.

"Thomas, this is all a mistake," Simon said.

Thomas stepped towards his brother and raised the sword again. His eyes showed that intelligent thought was not in residence. "You brought me here. You brought both of us here. For your little games."

"It wasn't me. I thought it was you."

"Liar." Thomas launched himself forward, the sword slashed down and across, each time Simon managed to move the shield in the way.

The clash of metal on metal echoed around the arena, the crowd above loved every sound and met them with their own cheers.

The Ringmaster leant over and whispered to Helena. "You have done well. They love this."

She smiled then peered down at the two combatants. A tinge of empathy floated across her consciousness but was soon chased away by the thought of how much wealth this fight would bring. The welfare of her family, of her people, outweighed the lives of two virtual strangers.

Simon slashed out with the spear, but Thomas jumped backwards away from the sharp tip. He stepped forward and slashed down on the upraised shield again, trying to force his younger sibling to his knees.

Simon held his ground. Thomas stepped to the side and hacked upwards, driving the sword into the bottom edge of the shield. It was ripped from Simon's grasp and went flying away out of reach. Simon was knocked to the ground and rolled away.

Thomas peered down at him. "Now you die. For all the pain and suffering you brought Helena, you will die," he said.

"But I haven't done anything, honest," Simon pleaded.

Thomas ran towards him, sword raised for one final slash at Simon. He leapt into the air, ready to cleave his brother in two.

Simon watched, incredulously, as his own flesh and blood came to kill him, and turned away. The spear tip rolled with him, pointing up at an oblique angle just as Thomas arrived.

The spear burst out of Thomas' back, forced through by the momentum of his body as he flew through the air. Thomas slid down its length and collapsed to his knees. Blood spewed from his mouth as he coughed on his own life-force.

Simon turned and saw the result. Horror and sorrow burst across his face. Tears welled and ran from his eyes as he screamed. "No."

He moved over to his brother and took him in his arms. "I'm so sorry, I'm so sorry," he said.

Thomas made no reply.

Simon looked up, beseeching the heavens. The smoke parted slightly, and his eyes were drawn to a solitary face in the crowd. "Helena," he whispered.

Thomas looked up. At the mention of Helena's name, a spirit grew inside him. He grabbed Simon by the throat and pushed him back. His rage-filled eyes stared deep into his brother's.

Thomas opened his blood speckled lips and said, "Yes, Helena," and drove his sword up through his brother's chest.

Simon fell backwards. His dying eyes peered up and beheld for the last time his one true love.

Thomas followed his gaze and managed to cast a glance at Helena before his own eyes glazed over and he saw no more.

The crowd erupted. They cheered and applauded as the Ringmaster made his way back to the podium.

"Friends, visitors, what a wonderful way to begin our Capricornia celebrations. Two innocent brothers driven to the edge—to each other's throats. Fighting until their last breaths, and all thanks to our latest Judas Goat, Miss Helena."

He held out his hands towards Helena. She stood and bowed to the assembled crowd. Those nearby patted her on the back and congratulated her.

As she sat down, the thoughts of riches and plaudits arose in her mind. *I think I could enjoy this.*

She scanned the crowd of happy and cheering faces. *Now, where do I find my next contenders?*

About the Author:

Stephen is an IT Geek, writer, actor, film maker and Taekwondo Black Belt based in Canberra Australia. He has been writing for over twenty years and has completed a couple of dodgy novels, sixteen feature length screenplays and dozens of short stories and scripts.

Stephen's scripts, TITAN, Dark are the Woods, Control *and* Death Spores *have found success in international screenwriting competitions with a win, two runner-up and two top ten finishes.*

His horror stories have featured in various anthologies including: Sproutlings; Hells Bells; Trickster's Treats #1, #2 and #3; Shades of Santa; Below the Stairs; Behind the Mask; Beyond the Infinite; Beside the Seaside; The Body Horror Book; Anemone Enemy; Petrified Punks; Beginnings; Sea of Secrets, Demonic Carnival; Deep Space; A Tribute to H.G. Wells; What If?; Through Death's Door and Coffins and Dragons. Over forty of his drabbles have been accepted by Blood Song Books; Black Hare Press; Fantasia Divinity and ThingsInTheWell.

Several of his Sherlock Holmes pastiches have been accepted for inclusion in anthologies published by Belanger Books and MX Publishing.

Later this year, Stephen will appear in the anthologies Journeys; Aquarius; Gemini; Pride; Bad Love and Jibbernocky. You can catch Stephen at his Facebook page https://www.facebook.com/stephenherczegauthor

CRAFT OF LIES

Maddie Jensen

There was prey on the Landsborough Highway. From his perch on the tin roof of a dilapidated petrol station, Roman zoomed in with his binoculars to observe his latest target. His lips curved into a smile. It had been weeks since they'd had any movement, so any acquisition was a welcome one.

"What've we got, Rome?" Her loaded harpoon tucked under her arm, Laura leaned in for an inspection.

"Ford Falcon." Roman set down the binoculars, squinting at the dust where the car was making its way toward them. "White. 2015 model most likely."

"Trying to make it to Capricorn Highway?" Laura smirked. "Good luck."

The ruins of Barcaldine sat upon the intersection of two highways, and that was where Roman and Laura targeted the automobiles.

They had preyed on trucks in the earlier days when The Wilds had been a more bountiful hunting ground. The parts on such large vehicles had kept the camps going for weeks, sometimes months. These days automobile movement was scarce, so they settled for cars whenever they could find them.

There was no way any of them were making the trip to a Metropolis to beg for help. They'd tried that a few years back, but The Devil had ushered them out of the closest Metropolis, Gracemere, and back into The Wilds. The Arcana wanted nothing to do with the peasants of the dangerous outside world, so Laura and Rome were forced to fend for themselves in the outback's scarred terrain.

"Get ready." Roman turned his attention back through the binoculars, and Laura scampered to the edge of the roof, positioning her harpoon. They were always the two the camp liked to send out, but sometimes a few others would come as well if they felt adventurous. Yet Laura and Roman were the Barcaldine camp's most dangerous because they were Crafters.

As the Falcon careened toward the trap at breakneck speed, something emerged from the dust behind it.

"Fuck, Roman!" Laura shot him an alarmed look over her shoulder. "That's a Metro jet."

"Stay focused," Roman said, although he too was unnerved by the jet's appearance. He and Laura were skilled Crafters. Laura was a skilled Mender, a Crafter with the ability to knit together torn flesh and broken bones. Roman was a Techie, rare in The Wilds, but prized for their ability to rip apart vehicles like this Falcon and put it together into something new to power their camps. However they had never dealt with a vehicle pursued by authorities. Scavenging wasn't technically illegal, yet it could get them both into a lot of trouble.

Laura sneered. "Knock it out of the sky."

He understood Laura's contempt—her parents had been consumed by the sickness spreading through The Wilds, the sickness that The Devil had ignored when they had begged for assistance. He had no more love for the Metros than her, but he didn't know what the consequences of bowling a jet out of the sky would be.

Closing his eyes, Roman concentrated. He focused his attention on the jet, bringing the engines to a halt.

Laura fired the harpoon across the road through a building just as the Falcon approached, forcing the driver to brake to a sudden halt. The car skidded out of control, colliding with the rope tied to the end of the harpoon that stretched across the highway intersection.

Roman was more focused on the jet, watching as it powered down. It took more energy than he'd cared to admit—he usually practised his Craft on smaller vehicles, not fancy high-tech Metro stuff. The jet crashed through the roof of a building that had once been an IGA. The plume of flames that erupted told him there was no chance of the pilot surviving, and that the parts would not be salvageable.

Down on the road, the driver of the Falcon rolled out of the car, slamming the door shut. A woman with dirty blonde hair planted her hands on her hips, chin jutting upwards as she examined the rooftop scavengers.

"You ruined my car!"

"Sorry, lady." Laura bounded from one rooftop to another before landing on the curb with the ease of someone who'd done this too many times. "I think we need it more than you do."

"Really?" The woman gestured angrily toward the burning IGA. "You don't think more of them will be coming? Now I've got to try and evade them on foot."

"Who are 'they'?" Roman asked as he followed Laura down at a more leisurely pace. He didn't think he'd ever seen Metro jets in pursuit of a civilian in an automobile. Whatever this woman had done, she'd managed to piss off the Arcana big time. She'd been headed in from the west—The Fool's territory.

"What does The Fool want with you?" Laura pressed, stepping forward to rummage around in the back of the car for anything of worth. The car itself was the prize, but they may yet find something else, something the woman was hiding. She didn't stop Laura, leading Roman to believe she didn't have anything important with her. Not a thief at least, then.

"The Fool's dead." The woman's blunt words made Laura pause in her movements.

"What?" Roman asked, although she'd been perfectly clear.

Perhaps it was the frequency of Arcana deaths lately that rattled him. The Arcana had ruled the ruins of Australia for generations. Powerful and territorial, they were overlords that sat in the Metropolises and looked down on The Wilds from their sparkling cities. There had been a time when the Arcana had inspired fear and respect.

Yet now their power was dwindling. It had begun two years before when someone had assassinated The Chariot. He was replaced as quickly as he had been killed, yet the idea that someone could assassinate a man with such authority was troubling. But The Chariot had only been the first—since then, The Magician and The High Priestess had also been taken out. Now it seemed The Fool was dead, too.

"Did you kill him?" Laura asked, her eyes glittering with delight at the prospect.

"No." The woman wrinkled her nose. She was younger than Roman had first thought, in her early to mid-twenties. "I'm actually headed to Gracemere. I need to see The Devil. I might not have killed The Fool, but I know who did."

"Oh really?" Roman was sceptical, unsure whether to believe her story. Would The Devil even listen to her? "Then why are they hunting you down?"

"It's a long story." The woman shook her head, exasperated. "I don't expect you to believe me, but I'd really prefer my car to get to Gracemere. It's a long way on foot."

Roman exchanged a look with Laura. They needed the automobile with a hunger bordering on desperation. Yet the woman needed it just as much as they did, if for very different reasons. He turned his attention back on the woman, considering her.

"What's your name?"

"Charlie." She raked her fingers through her tangled blonde hair. "Look, can I have the car back or what?"

"Not yet." It was Laura who spoke, slamming the car door and leaning against it. "You're coming back with us to the Barcaldine camp. We're not the one with the final say on whether we can relinquish our latest catch."

Barcaldine camp was one of the largest among the Capricorn Highway camps. It was more of a miniature city than a camp, a small town built from cars and trucks. They'd even managed to take down an old plane once, but that had been before Roman's time. The leader of the camp was Silver Pete, a feared and respected bandit with cybernetic limbs. Everyone was too scared to ask how he'd got them.

Thick plumes of smoke were visible from the highway, and Charlie's coughing at their arrival indicated her status as a newcomer. The locals were all used to the fumes from the fires.

"Roman. Laura." The affection in Silver Pete's voice was overshadowed by the greed in his watery eyes as he examined the car. "What have you brought us today?"

"Ford Falcon." Laura jammed an elbow into Charlie's back, nudging her forward. "Not to mention a prize to boot."

"A prize?" Silver Pete stepped forward to examine Charlie. He was somewhere in his fifties or sixties, grizzled and grey-haired. He had survived the sickness that had spread throughout The Wilds. Most who had caught it hadn't been so lucky, but Roman sometimes wondered if death just refused to take Silver Pete. He was too stubborn, and death had easier targets.

"She's from The Fool's territory." Roman folded his arms over his chest, realising by Charlie's stubborn silence that she wasn't going to be explaining. "He's dead. Fourth Arcana in two years. She reckons she knows who did it and that's why they hunted her."

"Who hunted her?" Silver Pete frowned, eyes fixated on Charlie. She lifted her chin but remained quiet, leaving the Crafters to do the talking.

Laura shrugged. "Rome took down a Metro jet. She must have pissed off some pretty powerful people there."

"You did what?" Silver Pete was incensed, eyes widening in horror.

Those were the unspoken terms: the people of Metropolises and The Wilds left each other alone, for the most part. Doing something like taking down a Metro jet violated those rules, and Roman realised for the first time what a stupid thing he'd done. He'd felt ecstatic at the time, a big hero taking down part of the unsympathetic government that cared nothing for outsiders. Now he realised what he'd done could be considered an act of war.

"It hardly matters now," Roman protested.

"Of course it matters!" Silver Pete snapped. "Do you think just because we're in The Devil's territory, he'll turn a blind eye?"

"It was the new Fool." Charlie's voice was soft, but the fact that she spoke at all took some of the heat off Roman, and for that he was grateful. "He's a tyrant. He was the one who killed his predecessor, and he accused me of being responsible. I had to run before I was sentenced to death."

"Why would he want you dead?" Silver Pete assessed her with a curled lip.

"Because he's afraid of what I know." Charlie took a deep breath, her eyes flicking across to Roman and Laura. "He's afraid because I've seen The Alchemist."

So she was a Seer, then. A Crafter, like Roman and Laura. Seers were few and far between, but all of them had seen The Alchemist. In the not too distant future, a man would rise who would banish sickness from The Wilds altogether, who would terraform the barren wasteland into something beautiful. The Seers spoke his name with reverence, as though he was some kind of god. Roman thought it was ridiculous, but he never said so aloud.

Laura scoffed. "The Alchemist is bullshit. A fairytale to make us feel better about a bleak future."

"No, it's not," Charlie protested. "I'm getting closer to finding out who he really is, but I need to go to Gracemere. To see The Devil. The new Fool might be challenged by what I've seen, but if I can talk to The Devil I can convince him of what's happened in The Fool's territory."

"Is this Alchemist in Gracemere, in the Metro?" Laura mocked, rolling her eyes and throwing Roman a look. "You don't seriously believe this, do you?"

Roman did. He couldn't explain why, but what Charlie said made a certain amount of sense. She'd been forced to flee The Fool's territory because she had seen something about The Alchemist that had scared him, and he'd tried to recapture or kill her when she'd left.

"We can use the Ford Falcon to get to Gracemere," Roman suggested, turning his gaze on Silver Pete. "Once we've delivered Charlie there, we can bring it back and strip it down for parts."

"Alright. But the car comes back here afterwards."

Roman and Laura exchanged a bewildered look. Laura's lips parted as though she wanted to say something, before she pressed her mouth into a firm line. Silver Pete was not known for making compromises.

A delighted smile curved the corners of Charlie's lips, the first sign of joy on her face since she'd met them, and Roman couldn't help but think how pretty it made her look.

Laura was a demon behind the wheel of the Falcon, dark auburn hair whipping around her as she sped along Capricorn Highway. Roman sprawled his lanky limbs across the whole back seat. Charlie was in the passenger seat, watchful and curious. It occurred to Roman that she wouldn't have seen The Devil's territory before. It was bleak, but Charlie regarded it all with something like wonder.

"You know we're asking to be hunted, right?" Laura's eyes flicked up to the rear-view mirror to lock with Roman's.

It was the truth—just as Laura and Roman had taken down the Metro jet and tried to take the Ford Falcon from Charlie, there would be others looking to do the same. Cars were scarce in The Wilds, and theirs would certainly attract unwanted attention.

Emerald camp would be the worst. Located on the intersection of Capricorn and Gregory Highways, they were one of the biggest threats in The Devil's territory—and their car would have to drive right by on the way to Gracemere, less than half an hour away.

"We have our abilities," Roman reminded her.

Laura scoffed. "You mean *yours*."

Roman's abilities were more useful in offensive situations, while Laura's Mender capabilities were typically utilised as a defensive measure. Still, Laura was a brilliant shot with her harpoon gun, rattling away on the floor in the back of the car. She didn't need to be a Crafter to be deadly, which was one of the things Roman admired about her.

People always suspected that they'd become a couple one day. It was probably because they'd been best friends since they were kids. Now as adults, they were Barcaldine's finest hunting duo. Roman and Laura, Laura and Roman. It seemed like an easy match. But Roman didn't feel that way about Laura, and he was sure she didn't either.

"You're awfully quiet," Roman glanced at Charlie, his comment, causing her to turn from the window. "Thinking about what you're going to say to The Devil?"

Charlie heaved a sigh. "Thinking about whether he'll listen."

Roman didn't see why he wouldn't. Charlie seemed to be a natural with people. Hell, she'd even convinced Silver Pete of the need to part with the Ford Falcon, even if only temporarily.

"Speak of the devil, and He shall appear." Laura cursed under her breath as they closed in on Emerald. There were sentries with rifles either side of the road, causing her to slow down and cast a look back at Roman. "Now what?"

"We're lucky they haven't attacked us," Charlie remarked.

"Lucky?" Roman laughed mirthlessly. "They're not attacking us because they want to show they don't have to.

One of the sentries tapped on the window. "Get out of the car."

Casting a meaningful look at the other two, Laura swung her door open and eased herself out of the vehicle, holding her hands up in the air to display her lack of weapons. Roman and Charlie followed her lead cautiously, while Roman's mind furiously ticked with ideas of escape. He was not a Crafter for nothing.

"What have we got here?" A greasy-haired man leered at them.

"Two girls, one boy." His companion's head was shaved near bald, and he waved a knife tauntingly in front of Laura's scowling face. "With a vehicle, too. Now, where were you lot going with that?"

"None of your business," Laura spat, and Roman tensed, hoping she'd just keep quiet. She was renowned for her temper and sharp tongue. It invited the sort of trouble they didn't need right now.

"Is that so?" The greasy man arched his eyebrows. "Maybe you won't share your reasons, but you'll be sharing your car."

"You will let us go on our way to Gracemere." Charlie's expression was like cold stone, and there was a power in her words that sent shivers running up Roman's spine. The greasy-haired man took a step back, and his near-bald companion looked disturbed. When Roman looked at Laura, her gaze was fixed on the harpoon in the car.

"All right." The greasy-haired man gestured to the car. "On your way, then."

Laura turned to glance at Roman, apprehension in her eyes. It shouldn't have been that easy in the slightest. The Emerald camp was known for being tough and merciless. Charlie's smile was indulgent as she slid back into the car, her ease with the situation indicating she knew precisely how it was going to go down.

They drove along in silence, neither Roman nor Laura daring to bring up the recent turn of events. The car finally broke down near Comet. Roman did his best to fix it, but he was a

Techie, not a Mechanic. The car was too old-fashioned for his power to work on, too reliant on fuel and grease instead of a Metro jet's electronics. In the end, he pronounced it dead, causing Laura to kick one of the tyres in a fit of temper.

"What the hell was that?" Laura demanded, turning her irate gaze on Charlie. "Back in Emerald, you just told those guys they were going to let us go to Gracemere and they left us alone. Did they know you?"

"No," Charlie responded, casting a wistful look down the highway toward Gracemere. "They responded because I gave them a command."

A sudden realisation felt like a cold trickle of water down Roman's back. "That's your Craft. You're a Wordsmith."

An uncomfortable silence fell over the trio. There hadn't been a Wordsmith in Roman's lifetime. They were rarely trusted because of what they could do—their words were poisoned honey, forcing those they spoke with to believe them, to obey them. A Wordsmith could convince the Arcana to turn on each other in an instant. Despite his budding feelings for Charlie, his palms were clammy and there was a knot tying itself tight in his stomach.

"So you lied." Laura was in front of her in an instant, slim frame tense. "You aren't a Seer at all, are you?"

"A Seer *did* tell me about The Alchemist," Charlie insisted, her eyes guilty and her expression apologetic. "But no, I'm not a Seer. Roman's right about me. I don't like using my ability at all, but I had to get us to The Devil. Using my gift was the only way to avoid violence."

"What was it the Seer told you?" Roman asked, curiosity overcoming him. "What did they see about The Alchemist that was so important?"

"I'll tell you in time, I promise." Charlie took a deep breath, her expression tender and her smile soft as she turned to him. "But first I have to get to The Devil."

"We can't trust her." Laura shook her head, her voice vehement. "She's already lied to us about what she is."

Charlie sighed, irritation colouring her tone. "Don't you think if I meant to mislead you, I would just have used my ability to make you forget what you saw in Emerald?"

Her power terrified Roman. The idea that all Charlie had to do was speak, and suddenly, people were completely under her control. He remembered tales of the Arcana hunting and killing Wordsmiths years ago. Some part of him could understand why. It made sense now why Silver Pete had been so agreeable, allowed them to take the car and head to Gracemere without argument.

"Regardless, looks like we're walking to Gracemere now." Laura's sour temper was beginning to improve, if only marginally. "It makes our trip a few days longer, but it's not impossible."

"Hey." Roman rested what he hoped would be taken as a comforting hand on her shoulder. "We've gotten through tougher situations than this."

Laura's responding smile was tight and didn't meet her eyes, but it was a smile nonetheless. Then she turned and began foraging in the back of the car. The harpoon was the first thing she removed. It was a hefty weapon, but Roman knew she'd never part with it—especially when she still considered Charlie a threat.

They scavenged Comet for any supplies. The town was among those bombed by the Metropolises when the sickness had first struck The Wilds, and amongst the ashes they managed to find canned food and camping supplies. They set up for the night, but Roman could feel the ghosts of the town watching him.

Comet had been among the settlements hit the worst, and there had been whispers of the sickness mutating into something monstrous there—which was what led The Devil to finally intervene. It had been the only action he'd taken with the sickness, to the anger of The Wilds.

Laura immediately clambered into her tent—harpoon by her side, as if she was concerned she might be attacked in the night—and bid them a sullen goodnight. Roman knew her mood would be better in the morning. Laura sometimes just needed time to sleep off her aggravation after a particularly trying day.

Not far away, Charlie lay on a blanket, arms clasped behind her head as she examined the stars. The closer they drew to the bright lights of the Metropolis, the fainter they appeared in the night sky. Roman collapsed beside her and for a few moments, they lay in companionable silence.

"Does it scare you? What's to come? The Alchemist?"

"No." A smile curved Charlie's lips, her eyes glimmering in the starlight. She turned her head to glance at Roman. "If it means a better world, I welcome him."

She was close enough that he could almost count the freckles on her cheeks. After barely a moment of doubt, Roman was overcome with a streak of boldness, pressing his lips to hers. Charlie responded with enthusiasm, their limbs and bodies tangling on the woven blanket as they found something in the middle of nothing.

Was this attraction based on desperation, on sensing a kindred spirit, on something deeper still? Roman would have time to dwell on it later, but right now he was caught up in the dangerous enigma that was Charlie. Wordsmith or not, he found that he trusted her. He believed in her.

They made love under the light of the crescent moon, the beginning of something both great and terrible.

Roman had never seen a Metropolis up close before. He hadn't been among the group who had previously travelled to Gracemere. There was no doubt that Gracemere was an intimidating sight. He could barely disguise his awe as he craned his neck back to examine the city's high walls, the skyscrapers that stretched up almost as high as the gloomy clouds above. Several jets flew in and out, the low rumble contributing to the general feeling of unwelcome. Gracemere was beautiful, but cold.

It was a place of bright lights and shadows—not to mention a lot of technology. Roman could feel it in the air, feel it nudging at his fingertips as though it begged to be used. How powerful his Craft could be here! What an irony that he came from The Wilds, when his ability was to control the technology his people lacked.

Laura's reaction was one of contempt. "They couldn't help cure the sickness, but they could afford to build themselves a fortress?"

Their arrival at the gates went without witness. Of course, in a place built like this, who needed guards? Charlie cast her gaze over the various panels and buttons, chewing thoughtfully at her lip.

"I could just break us in," Roman offered. The technology wouldn't be as simple as what he was used to, but he did enjoy a challenge.

"No." Charlie shook her head. "That wouldn't earn us any points with The Devil."

Roman shrugged his shoulders, but watched with avid interest as Charlie navigated her way around the system, pressing a particular button and speaking into a steel grill.

"Tell his Eminence that Charlie is here and wishes to speak

with him."

It took a few moments, but the gates ground open, just enough for two men to stride out toward them. Neither of them looked particularly pleased. Roman took note of their uniforms—coal-black with the symbol of the Arcana in gold. The cup, the pentacle, the sword and the wand. He could not remember the old tales about what they'd once represented, but now they only indicated the power of the Arcana.

"You are here to see The Devil?"

Charlie stepped forward. "Yes. I'm Charlie. You might not know who I am, but The Devil will hear me."

There was that icy feeling in the air again, the way her words seemed to resonate. Roman knew that Charlie was using her Craft on these men. It worked—how could it not?—for the guards exchanged a look before indicating for the small group to follow them.

Inside the Metropolis was even more brilliant than the outside. The buildings were all tall and glossy, as if entirely made of glass. Some of them probably were. The streets were orderly—no people sneaking down alleyways, no whispers or dealing in the shadows. It felt sterile, somehow wrong. Chills ran up Roman's spine as they entered the grandest building of all.

The Devil's home was not the largest of the skyscrapers in Gracemere, but it was easily recognisable by the same golden symbols that the guards had stitched onto their black uniforms. They glimmered in the light, and it almost felt like they were watching Roman as he stepped into a place he never thought he'd be allowed—The Devil's domain.

A man with slicked-back dark hair sat on a jet-black throne in the entrance hall. How like the Arcana, to believe they were kings—or even gods. Roman had heard many of them were Crafters, which explained how they were able to hold such immense power over the people of The Wilds. He rose, a vision in gold, a benevolent smile curving his thin lips.

This was The Devil.

He was tall and lean, although not quite as tall as Roman. As he strode over to them, Roman guessed The Devil was probably in his mid-thirties. There was something about the mirth in his eyes, the fond smile on his lips, which made Roman feel deeply uncomfortable. When he glanced at Charlie, she stepped forward and reached out a hand to them. The Devil took it and kissed the back of it.

"Rome," Laura whispered hoarsely, but he already knew something was wrong. Charlie and The Devil's greeting was not that of strangers. They knew each other. Why had Charlie lied, acted as though she didn't know The Devil? Had she been the one to kill the old Fool after all?

"I told you I could do it." Charlie sounded victorious as she tossed her blonde hair back, tilting her chin up proudly. "I said I'd bring them to you, and I did."

"Charlie?" Roman's voice was hesitant, but he knew a betrayal when he saw one.

There was something like regret in her eyes when she glanced at him.

"No. Not Charlie."

The Devil's laugh was delighted. "I can see you haven't made them aware of how the situation is changing. The Arcana has needed a cleanse for some time. The Chariot, The Magician, The High Priestess, The Fool . . . it needed to happen."

"You killed them?" Laura demanded to know.

Charlie shook her head. "Nothing so mundane. But in the next few days, there will be another death—and another successor."

"Why?" Roman asked. He'd never held any love for the

Arcana, but it sounded as though The Devil and Charlie—and perhaps others among them—were conspiring to murder and replace certain members. It didn't make any sense.

The Devil shrugged. "Because we need to ensure all of the Arcana will support The Alchemist."

The Alchemist again. Even the Arcana had such blind faith that whoever this man was, he would be able to save them, to breathe life back into a country long dead. It was almost a religion.

"Who is going to die?" Laura's voice was low, horrified. "Who is going to be the successor?"

The Devil took Charlie's hand in his own. "You stand before The Empress."

"Why did you really bring us here?" Roman asked, desperate to understand the full intricacies of whatever nefarious plot was being hatched in Gracemere. "You had a hand in The Fool's death and replacement. But why drag Laura and I into this?"

"You'll have answers soon." The Devil glanced at the guards. "Take him away. Make sure he's locked up securely."

"And the girl?" Charlie asked, her voice trembling.

The Devil's smile was dark. "Collateral."

"No!" Roman shouted, the same moment Laura raised her harpoon and levelled it with Charlie's head. Her teeth were bared and there was no sign of fear there. She would die as she'd lived—reckless and unafraid.

The Devil glanced at Charlie. "Make him do it."

"I . . ." Roman didn't understand precisely what The Devil had asked, but if Charlie appeared horrified by the command, it couldn't be good. Yet The Devil's fingers tightened around her wrist, a silent warning. There were tears glittering in her eyes, and Roman felt the shift in the air before she spoke.

"Charlie," he pleaded.

"Take the harpoon from her."

Roman did as instructed without a thought of rebellion. Laura's eyes widened in shock, but she couldn't move. Roman had heard rumours of The Devil being a telekinetic, a Mover, but he'd never seen the proof until now. When he glanced at the man, there was a malevolence he hadn't anticipated. He had thought The Devil ignorant, but this cruelty was far worse.

Charlie's voice shook when she spoke again. "Kill her."

"If you're going to do it, make it quick, Roman." Laura's voice was soft, her expression fierce.

Roman's fingers acted of their own accord, and the harpoon fired across the space between them, skewering Laura through the middle. She staggered back with the force of the impact, swayed, fell to her knees. Roman felt sick with guilt as blood poured from the wound. Laura raised her head and there was a defiant sneer on her face, her eyes full of hatred.

Someone was screaming, and it took him a moment to realise that it was him. Charlie was openly sobbing, as though she had the right to cry when she was the cause. This was what she had wanted—power. Her ambition had dragged her into this darkness, and he didn't feel sorry for her in the slightest.

Roman lunged for Laura, but the guards grabbed him by the arms, turning him away from the scarlet pool on the tiles and marching him from the hall.

It was some small mercy that he didn't have to watch her die.

Roman lost all sense of time in the darkness. The cell he'd been unceremoniously tossed into was what he imagined cheap accommodation would look like—basic furniture, and a small bathroom. His food was brought to him, and he suspected that both that and the water were drugged. In a place like this, he should have been able to use his Craft, but he couldn't—just as he hadn't been able to break free of Charlie's hold when she'd instructed him to kill Laura.

Not Charlie. She was not the young woman he thought he'd fallen for on the road to Gracemere. She was The Empress, cold-blooded and selfish, a creature he despised along with the rest of the Arcana. The only one of them he hated more than her was The Devil.

The door to his prison slid open, but for the first time instead of food and water, he had visitors. The Devil sauntered into the cell first, a smug expression on a face too angled and callous to be called handsome. The Empress followed, demure, resplendent in the gold of the Arcana. He could barely even recognise the woman who'd once been Charlie.

"How long have I been here?" he rasped, voice hoarse from disuse. "Why am I here? Laura was disposable, but you kept me. Why?"

"Your friend staggered off into the streets to die." The Devil waved a dismissive hand. "That was over a month ago now. We didn't find her body, but no one could have survived a wound like that."

Laura could have, Roman thought. He became hopeful despite knowing how dangerous that hope could be. Laura was a Mender. The wound was incredibly severe, but if anyone could have recovered, it was her. He forced himself to focus on other matters.

"I've been here over a month?"

"I brought you here because I was asked to." The Empress moved toward him, but Roman's eyes narrowed and her steps faltered. "It was my final test. Bring you to The Devil, prove I could be trusted, that I would do what I'd promised—and then I would become The Empress."

"Which you have." Roman's voice was cold. "You still

haven't said why."

"Because of The Alchemist." The Empress' eyes gleamed at the mention of him, their supposed future saviour. "Don't you see? Everything we've done is for his arrival. Making sure we have Arcana who believe in what he can do, who won't contest him."

"The previous Fool was a Seer." The Devil folded his arms. "Before his death, he saw more than just The Alchemist—he found out when The Alchemist would be born. He wanted to stop it, and that's when he was killed.

The Empress glanced at The Devil, then at Roman. "The Alchemist is born in the second week of January next year."

Roman did the maths in his head and found himself filled with a growing sense of foreboding. If The Empress was correct and he'd been imprisoned for over a month, then that meant it was currently early June, which meant . . .

"He's already been conceived."

"Yes." The Empress' smile was bright and genuine. "We had to be sure, because . . . Roman, you're The Alchemist's father."

A sense of dread settled over Roman like a heavy weight. The dots were beginning to connect. The reason why The Empress had manipulated him into trusting her, caring for her. Why they'd needed to keep him here to be certain. Why Laura had been expendable, but he hadn't been. The real reason why The Empress had been elevated to her position—a reason beyond her ruthless deeds.

"It's you," he whispered, staring up at her with absolute horror. "You're The Alchemist's mother."

The Empress pressed a hand to her stomach, still flat beneath the palm of her hand. The Devil leaned in to kiss her cheek. Roman wondered what sort of twisted relationship they had between them. There was no doubt in his mind that this was the man who would raise his son, who would take on the role of the paternal figure—who would perhaps even claim to be The Alchemist's father.

"So you're going to kill me now." Once, the idea would have scared him. Now, he felt resigned to his fate. Even if he hadn't been drugged, his full powers would be nothing against The Empress' Craft.

"No, you will live to see your son." The Empress' words were gentle, as though this was a consolation—a life of imprisonment instead of a swift execution. "Even play a part in raising him."

Roman shook his head fervently. "I won't condone this madness. I won't encourage him to grow up thinking he's some kind of saint. That's not the kind of reality I want for my son."

The Empress' smile chilled him to the bone. "Your reality is whatever I want it to be."

About the Author:

Maddie Jensen is a fantasy & science fiction author from Sydney, Australia. She has been reading and writing from a very young age, and is particularly invested in complex characters and well-written female protagonists.

THE PACT

Dee Cheers

"That's an interesting image." I pointed to the painting over the fireplace. "I don't think I've ever seen anything like it." The artist had depicted a mythical beast—part goat, part fish—set against an estuarine landscape of mudflats and wheeling sea birds. The overwrought baroque frame, all gilded cherubs and acorns, seemed at odds with the overt menace of the subject.

Iain laughed, handing me a glass of wine. I tried swirling it as I'd seen on the vid, nearly slopping it over my new dress.

"Yes, there's a funny story about that." His wine moved in glorious eddies of red and purple, without any conscious effort on his part. I could study etiquette for months and never achieve the careless perfection Iain and his family displayed.

I took a large gulp, hoping that sufficient alcohol might compensate for no class and little money. "So, tell me? I like a good story."

Iain cradled his glass and stared up at the painted beast. The fire crackled and spat, illuminating the planes of his face, accentuating sharp cheekbones and designer stubble.

"My ancestor, the first Lord Ambrose, had it painted." He raised the glass to his lips.

I watched, spellbound, as he swallowed.

"The legend is . . ." He paused, with a half chuckle. "The legend is that he gained these estates—and all his wealth—by making a pact with a sea monster."

"A sea monster." I moved closer to the fire, the heat warming my flesh. "I read that he gave King Louis the design for a new weapon. Demanded these lands as the price."

"Well, of course, that's the official story." He finished the last of his wine. "Our family is hardly going to tell everyone their ancestor made a deal with a monster to gain political advantage."

"And what did the monster get in return?" I turned, basking in the warmth of the fire. The mudflats are always so cold. The vaulted ceiling and painted frescos of the Great Hall soared above me.

"There, see, that's the funny bit. The legend is that the monster asked that in two thousand years, it could have one thing standing in the great hall."

"That's a bit obscure. That could mean anything." I really liked Iain. Unlike the rest of the family, he never intentionally made me feel less than them, just because I was poor and lived in a tiny village at the mouth of the river.

"I don't think my ancestor thought that far ahead. I mean, two thousand years. Anything could happen by then. It's far too long for anyone to worry about."

"I don't know." I put the glass back on the table. The crawling, shivering of the change raced under my skin. "It didn't seem that long to me."

About the Author:

Dee Cheers has been reading, watching and writing science fiction since childhood. Currently writing her first full-length novel, she describes writing as the most frustratingly rewarding thing she has ever done.

In real life, her work takes her to some of the most remote areas of Australia. Dee lives in Brisbane, with a dog and two cats.

CAPRICE

Brianna Bullen

When he was born under a red-smeared night sky, directly beneath the arrow-headed constellation of his kind, they said he was blessed. An intelligent boy, the mid-Doebhean (the mid-wife) told his Buckathair as she clipped the tag into his child's flailing ear. The young buck had been gifted with strong ears that would be perfect for listening to and navigating the river's currents. Strong antlers too for defending the herd.

They did not say he was born of misfortune—did not comment on the dying bleats of his Doemathair that still reverberated in his astute ears, nor on the blood that coated her humanoid face and matted pelt from where his over-developed horns had torn her canal open.

His Buckathair took him in his broad arms, holding his small progeny with the same awkward delicacy with which he held his artisanal craft projects. It was as if this creation was yet another piece of art, a collaboration with his beloved Doebhean, his beloved Clheam—their masterpiece. The mid-Doebhean left as soon as she'd handed the baby to his Buckathair. He wrapped the child more securely in his arms, kissing the blood-congealed fur on his forehead. The baby would not stop crying. All he could do was rock it gently, hold it close for warmth, giving it the illusion of still being safe in the womb. He chewed on a bit of hay, masticating it into a paste for the bundle's consumption.

The thing just bit his finger and huffed. The mid-Doebhean had rushed out claiming to need to haggle for milk from another brooding Doemathair. He was alone, the body of his wife splayed across the coach with their pelt-skin blanket draped over her eyes. The baby was shivering, but he didn't have the strength to take the blanket off his wife to swaddle the kid yet. He was gasping for air just thinking of her, but he couldn't panic for his child's sake. The kid was still bleating tears, however they were getting weaker, sleepier. He looked down at the bundle, as if the Buckid in his arms could give him a solution to his aching turmoil and bitterest joy. It stared back with eyes not clouded by sleep, but with an understanding and acceptance unbefitting of its age. Those square pupils were eclipsed with tragedy where the clarity of innocence should have been. The yellow of his Doemathair's irises a tarnished gold in his own.

The matriarch of his herd stopped by to bless his Doemathair, the strong cloven hooves of her lower body clacking on every level of the practice-run stairwell his wife had prepared for the baby. The matriarch did not knock—it was not her due. She entered with her broad face held high, her shoulders back straight, and her steps sure. Her posture loosened completely as her nostrils slitted further upon taking in the blood and shit on the air.

"Clheam?" Her uncanny pupils swivelled to the body of the doe on the couch.

"She is gone."

"Ah." The herd matriarch's face betrayed nothing, ever the stern mask of negotiations, but the sureness of her steps were slower, left flank shaking minutely as she walked to the body. Lifting the blanket, she nuzzled and snuffed the sweat of the dead woman's hair-fur, giving it a single kiss before turning to the new Buckathair. Her eyes locked on the trembling kid. Blood and a string of flesh still dangled from his left horn, not yet curved with maturity but disturbingly shaped and sized. She had never seen such large horns on a child. Usually they grew with the child from stumps in the skull, but this baby's were already two, almost three inches tall.

"Buckid or Doekid?" Her raspy voice was even, a poker-voice.

"Buckid."

She nodded. "There have been many this season." She took a small wooden toy from her belt pouch—a sling-shot shaped as a fish tail—and hung it on the doorhandle. "For the kid. Congratulations for your joy. My deepest condolences for your loss."

The trout moved as liquid over the rocks, a waving form, only differentiated from the water by colour. Aren leapt up on one of the dry rocks by the bank, hooves skidding in his haste. "Bhear, there!" Milky blue eyes followed the path of the water, pointing at a rock in the centre of the shallow river, slate grey blackened by water's caress. "There's a whole school coming, get on that middle rock!"

Bhearen nodded, his horns glistening near-silver in the sun. Sweat trickled down his bare chest from their morning foraging pursuit, catching between his pectoral muscles. Standing tall and broad, he was a magnificent specimen of a buck, backlit and casting a similarly sure shadow. Few would have been able to tell of his birthing difficulties, if not for the almost antler-like horns grazing the sky.

"No need to pose and show off, my good friend Bhear, no doe, nor Buckathair, nor Matriarch to impre—oh Capricorn, here we go again."

Bhearen leapt high in the air, in a blissful arc. His cloven hooves landed strong, adjusting slightly over the rock without slipping on the saturated surface. He threw a smile at his companion, which would have come off as cocky from any other buck and yet Bhearen made it come off as puppy-dog earnest. A 'were you watching, I can't believe I just did that' smile.

He responded to Aren's eyeroll by diving a hand underwater, fingers cutting through like the blade of a heron's beak. The fluid motion flicked several fish out of the water, the sun glistening over the spotted scales on their sides. Aren sat down on the rock, mentally going over the route back home to calm himself. He was tense, but the way back felt ingrained and this soothed all anxiety surrounding not getting the required amount of fish for the ceremony. His eyes glanced up to see if Bhearen had noticed his boredom, but his scouting partner was a picture of perfect concentration, now plucking fish from the water with optimised energy-conserving movements. A soft smile was on his face.

Aren sighed and plucked a handful of weeds by the base of his rock to chew on. Bhearen struggled with a particularly wily fish who was not going down without a fight. It slipped out of his wet fingers, slapped against his stomach, and nearly fell back into the water. Bhearen lashed his hand out, grabbed it, and brained it against the rock before it could react. With a deep sigh, he dropped it on the impressive pile of fish he'd gathered, wiping the sweat from his brow and scratching at the wet fur at the base of his ear. There was a reddening wet imprint on his stomach from the last fish's escape attempt.

Aren smiled at the absurdity, eyes latching onto the way the water slowly trickled down taut abdominal muscles, catching in the divots before sliding into the damp fur beneath his waist. Show off. All topped off with two large horns, slightly curved and powerful and perfect for fighting. His own singular natural horn couldn't compete. He couldn't compete even when he had two, their play fight skirmishes always ending with Aren yielding and walking off to clean his wounds and settle until the noise of their clash had faded from his ears. Now with only one, and the other a purely aesthetic replacement that would bend and shatter under any real pressure, he could never compete again.

"Thirteen fish for the ceremony, Aren!" said Bhearen.

Aren shook his head, brushed down dust from his hide and crossed his arms. "Show off." He tried to ignore the way the water splashes on those strong shoulders caught the sun. Bhearen was always the golden boy, yet Aren was glad to be chosen as a friend. His mouth felt cotton-ball dry—guilty jealousy tasted of moths.

The walk back to town was quiet. Aren kept looking down to his hooves, then back at Bhearen, trying to clamp down on jealous words. Bhearen just looked at the trees, goofy smile in place and a spring in his step. His tail trembled with glee when he saw a startled chipmunk—its cheeks fattened with hibernation—running along a tree branch, and again when he heard the trickle of a nearby stream. Bhear dashed off to follow the sound, grabbing the curve of Aren's remaining natural horn and tugging him along. The stream was running strong between moss-covered rocks. Wildflowers opened their mauve petals into stars on a sky of green and brown. In the centre of one flower, a flying insect hummed, carrying a handbag of pollen behind its legs. Bhearen's wide eyes turned to Aren in complete delight. "Aren! Is that a bee?"

The noise startled the insect, which stopped its delicate

rounds and flew away. Aren watched it go with much less sorrow than his friend. There was little hope of seeing a true bee in the wild. Pollination occurred artificially these days, a troupe of experts going out each day to ensure the necessary process was done. What once occurred naturally in nature was now done with carefully calibrated machinery. "Probably just a fly."

"Then how do you explain the pollen packs?"

"Maggots. Growing from under its parent's arms. Eating it alive."

Bhearen leant over to drink from the fresh water, cupping his hands and taking a long sip. "Creepy."

Aren snorted, the water jolting through his nostrils.

Bhearen chuckled heartily as he slapped his friend on the back, the force causing his new cybernetic leg to slip in the soft ground and almost become bogged. Bhearen helped him up, wiping down the mud off his legs and between his two toes with his hands. The metal toes pulled inwards, designed for flexibility and movement.

"It's a bit uncanny, isn't it? That they move?" Aren's hands fidgeted in his hair, looking away.

"Nah dude, it's heaps cool. Must come in handy for gripping into the ground."

"I guess. Just takes a bit to get used to." Aren's eyes narrowed in on Bhearen's twitching fingers. "Tell anyone I'm ticklish and I'll impale you on your own horns."

Their walk back was less tense as they followed the windy trail back to their herd. Aren stopped occasionally to graze at the thin grasses, digging away at the flat snow that had packed in over the ground. He found a tube—rhizomic and fat with nutrients—rooted into the ground, and gave it to Bhearen.

"Share it with your Buckathair."

The higher altitude was felt in the thinning of the air and the increasing vastness of white. They could hear nothing but their own steps as they drew closer to town. Weaving through the skeletal lodgepole pines on the outskirts of town, the trees looked like frostbitten leg bones sprouting from the ground.

Aren relaxed as they came to the cleared path leading into town. Tacky Christmas tinsel, and a sign saying 'Welcome to Herdon' were draped over the single limber pine on the path. Split and worn down by time, the tree was forked like a snake's tongue. The leaves on its branches had long been dashed away by the wind, but it remained rooted in the ground. Aren looked to his friend, wanting to know if the tree's stubbornness brought him the same amount of comfort. Bhearen's jaw was set. His shoulders and neck shifted into a firm line, as if a lodgepole had lodged itself in his spine. He let out a long breath. All the puppyish joy of the foraging mission was gone, not even a ghost of it remaining in his haunted expression.

The outskirts of town were silent. As they moved further down the track, they passed a wooden home with opened blinds at the top of its elevated stairwell and saw a flicker of another being inside. They heard the baying laughter of the town's comedian, Jaela, bouncing down the street, ricocheting off other houses. The steady hum of the light-posts was no match for the iconic laugh of the comedian, no doubt practising for the festival. The sun had almost set, the dark settling over the town like a bruise. The path was lit by light-posts and lamps, glowing white like hovering snowballs. Aren watched his friend become engulfed by his own shadow which walked on the wall behind him.

Bhearen held the bucket of fish against his upper leg, as if unbothered that the stench would absorb into his fur. Aren cleared his throat, and it must have sounded dry and pained, as

Bhearen immediately offered him his cloak. Aren tried not to feel weak. Again. Bhearen was being kind, but he couldn't help but fear it came from a place of pity. He hated relying on his friend.

"It's not a cold. Anyway, you must be freezing after all your water aerobics earlier. How are you not dead, anyway?"

"Buckathair says I was born into an icy world with blood made to meet it. I don't feel the cold."

Aren shook his head as snow escaped the eaves of a house and fell onto him. "So your ear tag never gets that metal iciness that feels like you're going to freezer burn alive? Lucky prick."

"I think my great-great-great-great-however many greats may have been editing their blood a little bit more than the usual. My Doemathair was notorious for volunteering for recovery missions in the winter."

"Do you think they'll be happy with the fish offering?" asked Aren, changing the subject.

Bhearen nodded. "I think they're just happy the waters down-mountain haven't completely frozen over."

When they arrived at the town centre, there were three things that made Bhearen pause: a group of people clustered around Theremon's seed shop; the Matriarch standing on an orator's podium, her curved horns gleaming with healing oil; a carving of Capricorn hanging from the square's quacking aspen, already framed in a peppering of snow.

In the centre of the group was a doe not much younger than their own nineteen winters, smiling sheepishly as she ran her hands through a bag of seeds. Matrina was standing, ears lowered, feet scuffing at the ground in the perfect display of contrition. As the daughter of the Matriarch, she shouldn't have been sneaking around. Should have been setting an example. But she was still just a child, and a child who liked shiny things and had a sweet tooth for seeds and strange information. Bhearen wondered if she been caught stealing pumpkin seeds again. He ran over the rocks shaped into cobblestones to get closer to his friend and failure of a thief. Aren rolled his eyes and took his time, stopping in front of Doe-Ma Ann's store to check out her stock of scented kindling. He'd heard Matrina getting chewed out for similar thefts in the past; he didn't need to listen to another lecture. She certainly wasn't going to.

Bhearen caught the tail-end of the reprimand, surprised to hear nothing of pumpkin seeds and sticky grazing. Rather, Theremon had moved on and was not ranting about their frustration over insufficient sales, a speech that seemed to not actually be directed at Matrina except for the tacked on "and it doesn't help that there are people like you with sticky fingers." The girl wasn't listening anyway, staring off into the distance, lost in her own thoughts—not even Bhearen's friendly wave could snap her out of it.

"Matri," Aren yelled across the square, interrupting Theremon who muttered about loud children and stopped paying attention to either of them. Aren came towards them with two cones of shaved ice. A smile that didn't look uneasy unless you knew him well. Matri jolted as if she'd done something wrong and was ready to bolt. "Relax. Do you need a moment to yourself? Want to come walk by the lodgepines? We saw some birds earlier. The thrush kind."

Matrina blinked, her awareness slowly returning to the market square. Her nostrils wrinkled. "Ain't that a venereal disease?"

"Not quite that serious." Aren started walking off, indicating with a cock of his head for Matrina to follow. "Are you going to report to your Doemathair and let her know you got caught thieving and repent like a good citizen, or will you come with us?

"Come with you guys, a hundred percent."

"I got you a berry mix ice, isn't that your favourite?"

She pulled a face. "I'm pretty sure that's your favourite. Don't know why, all those bittersweet lumps are so gross."

"You take that back. The lumps are great, right Bhear?"

Bhearen was watching the Matriarch, her fur-hair long and greying, and her face pinched in concern. A pair of Capra Corps scouts were speaking to her in hushed tones, much to the chagrin of her advisors. One of the scouts, his eyes masked with wind-protecting glasses, lifted his head away from the Matriarch's ear and made direct eye contact with Bhearen. He jumped.

"Bhear?" said Aren.

Bhearen blinked, returning to the expectant, waiting silence of his friends. "You going to back me up, buddy?"

Bhearen smiled sheepishly and shrugged. "I'll back you up if we can take the fish to Buckathair or Matri's Doemathair. Got to get these fish to their life's purpose."

Aren cocked his head. "That's a great point. Have you seen your Buckathair at all or should we interrupt the frankly terrifying Matriarch—no offence Matri—"

"None taken, she scares me too."

"To tell her we've got the fish ready for the Hunt?"

"I haven't seen my Buckathair in weeks," Bhearen admitted. "He's been in one of his moods. Working on something big, I feel."

"As big as your horns?" Aren reached up to tug on the left one, smiling at Bhearen's scowl. "I can't help but feel those were the most incredible things he made."

Matri whistled innocently. "Probably shouldn't be checking out his horns while I'm here. I don't want to hear your flirtations."

"I wasn't—not with—shut up, I'm just teasing." Aren let go of his horn regardless.

"Right," Matri grinned but left it at that.

Bhearen honestly felt a little flustered himself. Tried not to get his hopes up and returned to his proper thoughts. "I mean, knowing Buckathair it wouldn't surprise me if the horns were one of his inventions. Bit of gene-splicing on an embryo here and there. Wouldn't put it past him." Bhearen fought down the bitterness. It would have been just like his Buckathair. Short-sighted 'look what I can do' experimentation on an unborn son with a long-term cost to his Doemathair.

Aren shuddered. Matri's smile dropped.

Bhearen remembered his smile. Turned it to them. "I mean. That's just a theory I thought of in one of my darker turns towards him. It's probably not real."

Matri murmured, "I heard a similar rumour in town though."

"See? Might have been how the thought came to me. Hearing something and not registering it until later to the point I took it for my own thought. It was probably just someone trying to slander him. It's happened before. Will probably happen again."

Aren interrupted. "He's done a lot of good around her though. Both with his craftsmanship and his scientific work. I've been told we wouldn't be as well off as we are now without your Buckathair's ingenuity."

Bhearen smiled minutely. "Thanks. But I don't need any reassurance about my Buckathair. He's a tough man, he can handle himself." He did find his smile growing though in thanks as he looked at his best friend.

Aren smiled back, genuine and soft. "I wouldn't defend him if I didn't think he was worth defending."

Bhearen's eyes glanced to Aren's artificial horn, noticing his friend grow tense as his eye tracked over it. Aren's natural horn's keratin caught the light in stratified patches. The other was moulded out of metals and plastics, the light running along it in an uninterrupted line. It was unnaturally smooth, but from a distance could at least afford Aren the illusion of being a competitive buck. Bhearen's Buckathair had made it for him after the accident, partially to keep the frostbite out and partially for his friend's self-esteem. Bhearen personally thought it was quite a nice, sturdy horn with a pleasant curve that matched Aren's natural horn, and it wasn't just because his dad made it that he admired it. While the memories of injuring his friend haunted him, the horn itself reminded Bhearen that Aren was still here, was still a survivor.

Bhearen had fallen into the object of his contemplation, rubbing his finger down the carved ridges and along the curve of Aren's horn. "I don't know how you can forgive me."

Aren jerked away, his ear twitching underneath it in overstimulated annoyance. "Not your fault. It was mine for challenging you. Again. Just youthful stupidity."

Bhearen could sometimes hear their heads crashing together, just so, brains ricocheting against their double-layered skulls. Blood and a surprising amount of testosterone-kindled dopamine were rushing behind his eyes. They'd come together, body wrangling against body, head slamming against head, again and again, as all males did during ruts in the mating season. Theirs had been practice between friends though, not intending to wound or break neck or skewer. Mucking around. That was why the accident had happened.

Blood geyser-gushing against the snow, beside a fallen place marker pinecone. His horns, those goddamn destructive antler-like life-ruining bastards, lodged into the skin just at the base of Aren's horn. Penetration shattering the bone growing in his horn, luckily not penetrating fully through the skull. Surgeons having to carefully dislodge them, as if untangling a jigsaw puzzle. Aren refusing to allow them to saw through Bhearen's offending horn too, even though it would have made removal easier.

Aren's screams were muffled by a ripped off sleeve shoved between his teeth as they sawed the damaged and half-dislodged horn down to the bone.

The gap between them. The hole in his head.

The fever brought on by infection—Aren flushed, sweat caught in his dark hair-fur dribbling down his browline, eyes glassy and faraway. Bhearen had never wanted to cause him pain. Pus and the occasional leak of blood sent a chill down Bhear's body every time he sat by Aren's bed.

"We . . . we should get going." Bhearen shook his head. Whipped snowflakes from his eyelashes. "The weather can probably keep them from spoiling, but I think our hides will be had if we don't bring them in time for the ceremony to start."

They walked in silence until it was broken by Aren's pondering. "What happened with old Buck Theremon anyway? Thievery doesn't usually bring such a big crowd."

Matrina ignored his question. "I take it you are both participating in the Torthe ceremony this time? You're old enough now."

"So are you."

Matrina giggle-snorted. "Me, being touched? Not in my interests. Besides, there are way more than thirteen who can participate this year, and I'm not fighting to be a part of that bloodbath."

Aren snorted. "Please. It won't be a bloodbath. Ol' doe Matriarch will make us draw straws if there are too many volunteers. No blood on her snow."

"Neither of you are being fair; to Matriarch or the ceremony. It's—it should be beautiful."

Aren nudged Bhear. "Maybe to the big, handsome golden boy. Have all those beautiful does fawning over you, wanting to have your kids and potent pen—"

Matrina covered her ears. "Someone sounds a bit jealous."

Aren sidestepped over a fallen branch. "Of Bhearen? Not ashamed to admit it. Who wouldn't be?" He made a sweeping motion down his own body. "Can't exactly compete in the whole 'virile warrior with a heart of gold and tenderness of a lamb' department."

Bhearen's blinked at him in disbelief. "Is that all you think of me? Someone to compete with?"

Aren shook his head. "Not at all! I'm just saying in the romantic department, you're swoon-worthy and I'm kind of . . . not."

Bhearen frowned. "What are you talking about? You're one of the strongest people I know—the canniest too. You always keep your fur and hair-fur in such great condition. It shines like stars in midnight when the light goes through it. Like, how do you get all the burs and tangles out? I've heard several does comment on it, I swear."

"Does." Matrina coughed into her fist. "Stars in midnight? The fuck does that mean? Please stop with the lovefest already."

Aren leapt over to her, putting on a voice that sounded like the perky town motivational speaker. "Oh but Matrina, your speed with a saw, your ability to pickpocket and see patterns, your little black bob and plump tail stripe—why, you're the one to get all the bucks and does fluttering and swooning."

Matrina rolled her eyes. "They can swoon all they like. I'm not interested in their pelts. The fluttering is probably angina and they should see a doctor."

"Do you think it'd mess things up if I took away a few fish tails? Lowered the numbers of participants?" Matrina asked. "I mean it's all tradition and all that, thirteen fishes for our thirteen successful forebears and all that shit. Twelve for the months, an extra for the continuation beyond that. But surely we can all do without more ceremony kids running around. Everyone conceived on this night is just so . . . snobby."

Aren chuckled. "Weren't you a ceremony kid?"

"Yeah we don't talk about that." Matri sniffed the air.

"Too good for the kids who think they're too good for us?" Aren teased.

Bhearen shook his head, smiling and looking up at the sky, taking in the red tinge left by sunset. He felt uneasy but wasn't sure if it was at the bloody sky or Aren's apparent flirtations.

Fireworks went off in the distance. The smell of sulphur hit the air. The chemical reaction in the sky blazed into a flower, streaming away into tiny falling stars. Matri flinched and hunched over. "Shit that was loud. Does anyone feel like there's something in the air? Not just smoke or sparks or nitrate—"

"Pheromones?"

She cringed. "No. I just have a really bad feeling about things."

Bhearen spoke lowly. "I did see a lot of movement around your Doema—the Matriarch. Do you know what's going on?"

Matri's expression became pinched. She looked down at a patch of grass on the ground and kicked at it until it dislodged. "No. I figure it's just ceremony stress, but there are things happening that just don't align with that. More tension than a simple celebration." She bit her lip. "I really don't like it."

"Do you need us to take you home? Or at least to my Buckathair's workshop? There's a spare key inside the dirt of the pot-plant, in-case things are bad with your Doemathair at the moment."

"It's surely not that bad," the Matriarch's voice cut blade-clean through the air. Her shadow loomed over them as she stood at the entrance to town, cutting them off. She was a tall woman—taller even than Bhearen—with a severely lined face and sagging shoulders. Still, she stood proudly, a knowing glean in her brown eyes which darted from face to face. Her half-opened bomber jacket flapped heavily in the wind. "You young kids have dawdled enough in your duties. I seem to recall we have a matter of fish to discuss."

Bhearen reached down to grab the thrown fish. He unstrapped the bucket from his back and handed it to the Matriarch, who received it with firmness. Bhearen slumped, knowing that they should have gotten the fish set up at the starting line of the Torthe ceremony by now. Air hissed out her nose as she breathed out and leaned over to whisper in his ear. "More important than fish or any frolicking—it's about your Buckathair. Where is he?"

Bhearen felt the anxiety rising within him, and he wasn't quite sure why. Pieces weren't quite slotting together, leaving gaps to go along with his unease. There were no answers for his for the question of where his Buckathair was, nor why his disappearance irritated him like a tick on the skin. He tried to recall if his Buckathair had said anything about what he was working on. "When was he last seen?"

"You don't know?"

"Buckathair has been acting weird lately. I just assumed he was onto some new experiment. He'd been holing himself up in his workshop for weeks, and then he just disappeared. Haven't seen him for weeks."

"And you weren't alarmed?"

"It's happened before. He just ups and leaves and then turns up a month down the track as if nothing has happened. But—"

"Yes?"

"He's been more tense lately."

"You've noticed too?" The Matriarch smiled.

"I'd be a terrible son not to." He smiled back; the movement was forced. "Something hasn't been right for months."

They took the conversation back to the town-square, in whispers and quick glares at anybody official or otherwise who walked to close. The horns of her predecessors dangled from the Matriarch's jacket and clanged with each step. Bhearen did not take his eyes off the Matriarch as she filled him in on the mundane details of dealings with his dad and frustrations over the festival preparations. Their fish weren't as late as Derride's famous seed pastries—an oven malfunction—the ceramic artist's goat statue, or even the communal blankets for the crowd which were to be wrapped around the shoulders of the new lovers to return from their Torthe. "I've sent some officials over to find your Buckathair—in the meantime, I would suggest finding a place near the starting line for the beginning of the Torthe. The thirteen boats have already been set-up by the entrance of the river. If you could be there to hand out the fish to any of the participants, it might be easiest. They will no doubt inform you if any of you have been selected. You young folk should not concern yourself with the stresses of the old."

"But it's my Buckathair you're looking for," Bhearen protested.

"And we hope to find him," the Matriarch said firmly.

The group sobered as they walked past Mr Trelorn's house, its two storeys collapsed into each other like a shoved-in accordion, the tiles of its roof scattered over the pavement like giant fingernails.

"When did this happen?" Bhearen looked to the Matriarch.

She sighed. "Yet another incident at this time to give me wrinkles."

"Was it ransacked or . . ."

"Matriarch, this really can't wait." An official approached, tugging someone behind him, tied up with rope. A stranger.

The stranger was dressed to blend in with the mountain, and this stood out in the town. Their hair was the colour of slate rock and tied in a low ponytail; their cloak was a speckled granite, dotted with snow and large splashes of blood. Their legs were long, the fur smoother than the shag of their community, and ended in a single hoof. But the strangest, most uncanny part of this stranger was their tail—a long, tapering, trout-like protrusion slapping the ground with each step like some mockery of the Torthe ceremony. During the Torthe, young lovers would tie a fish behind themselves like a tail, chasing each other down river and across country to pluck the fish for their consumption and make a pact for mating, sharing the last bite. The creature was a warped vision of the Capricorn, like the carving in the centre of the village square.

Capricorn, the saviour. Had their forebears not been merged with goats, they would not have adapted to the mountains. Would not have survived the floods of the old lands below. The transformation took place during the period of Capricorn, a good omen if ever there was one.

This monster was not the Capricorn they celebrated.

Its shrewd eyes darted between faces, lingering on Bhearen's, documenting everything it saw with an unshielded arrogance. On its head were antlers even longer than Bhearen's, broken off into branches.

Bhearen stepped forward, curious. "Who are you?"

The stranger looked at him and spat on the ground. "I know your face; it is one we curse."

"What do you mean?"

The Capricorn creature sneered. "Your dear Buckathair's been interfering with things he shouldn't be."

"What does—?"

The stranger tapped its lips, going silent with a smirk.

Matrina smiled at the Matriarch. "Another thing to add to the growing list of problems for the festival, huh? Not as bad as the rising sea-levels."

The Matriarch turned on her, nostrils flaring. "Go home, Matrina. I don't want to see you right now if you're not even going to participate in the Torthe. You're just going to get underfoot, as you always do, you sneak."

Aren and Bhearen shared a glance. "Honestly, maam," said Aren, "we're happy to have her with us, even if she doesn't want to participate in the festivities—"

"She's going to her beloved workshop. End of discussion." The Matriarch stared Aren down.

Matrina walked up the stairs and out of the square without a backwards glance.

"Matri, wait," said Bhearen.

Aren shook his head, ears fluttering in agitation under his antlers. "Give her time to lick her wounds."

The stranger was chuckling, the sound gravel to the eardrums. Aren shivered—the chill of the night seemed to be setting into his bones. Bhearen couldn't feel anything.

The Matriarch turned her ire onto the stranger. "Yes, parenting can be very funny." She said, dry as stone. "Almost as funny as trespassing."

The stranger, if anything, laughed louder. "And yet you do nothing when one of your own trespasses on our land. Experiments on my people to save your own."

The official tugged them towards the informal holding cells, mainly used by youth in the community who needed to sleep off embarrassment, and those with existential despair who needed monitoring overnight.

The Matriarch signalled for him to stop. "Make sure it gets some tea, food and a blanket. I'd tend to it now, but it is the hour of Capricorn's vivacity and must get these bucks—and the ceremonial fish—into position for their chase."

"Very well, Ma'am."

Bhearen watched the strange creature until it entered the holding cell, despite Aren's insistent tugs at his hand. He turned on the Matriarch. "What did that Buck mean?"

"Bhearen it's not really anything you should concern—"

"It concerns my Buckathair doesn't it? So it concerns me."

The Matriarch let out a long sigh. "There have been sightings of other beings along the outskirts of town for many decades now. At first we thought they were just rumours, but we sent scouting parties out to make contact. Propose trade. Your Buckathair was among the first dispatch. As a self-proclaimed 'builder' of things he came bearing trinkets. Both wooden and biotechnological. Little artificial lives. It wasn't a show of power, but a show of skill. To convince these people we were worth being in contact with. They weren't—they aren't like us, not from the first Thirteen. But an offshoot done to survive lower on the mountain. Ones that can swim as well as climb."

"I've never seen anyone from outside of town before," Bhearen whispered.

"We didn't know there were any other survivors on this mountain for so many years. We thought it would be a miracle.

Only they're immunity is . . . low. They get sick easily. Your Buckathair and some of the more scientifically-inclined among my cabinet have been working on medicines. But no luck. They have been growing only weaker. More angry."

"He looked like . . ."

"Yeah."

"Buckathair always showed me photos, but I've never seen anyone but Doemathair with horns as large as mine."

Bhearen's head felt heavy. "If Doemathair was part of a group lower on the mountain—or even off the mountain—why are we so alone? Can we leave the mountain, or are we stuck up here forever?"

The Matriarch pursed her lips. "We're trying to figure that out. None of our ship scouting parties have returned in fifty years. It's best not to get hopes up."

"So there's possibly more to this world out there? More than high altitudes and the frost my friends feel?"

She turned her stormy gaze to him, square pupils pinning him in place. "Your adaptations would make you unlikely to survive out there."

"But there's a world out there?"

She sent him off not with direct words, but by turning away. She spoke up again only when she heard him start to shuffle off. "We will keep you updated on your Buckathair."

Bhearen stumbled off, Aren supporting his friend's weight and righting him before he tripped. The taller Buck startled back to himself. "There's . . . there's a world out there. Do you think there's a world out there?"

Aren sighed, pinching his brow. "I don't know, Bhear. I'm in the same boat as you. Heck, normally I'd want to know more too, but honestly I'm tired and just want to eat and sleep.

Possibly partake in the third pleasure at the Torthe, if I'm honest."

Bhearen blushed, his whole face going red up to his hairline and beneath his tufty side-burn. "Aren, you can't just say that."

"For someone who loves showing off their physical prowess, you're awfully bashful."

"Because that's private!"

"What if it's in public?"

"Then it's illegal."

"Outside the Torthe."

"Well yeah, but if it happens then it's not actually *in* public . . . You're distracting me, aren't you?"

"Yup."

Bhearen hunched in on himself, his tall frame condensing seemingly into half the space.

"Not talking about it doesn't make it go away, I know."

There were artificial lights strung up by the time they had returned to the main square. These were made of carved glass, which reflected the moonlight back through the square at this time of the year. The central erected podium had its own lights twined like vines along its pillars. Above it, a woven straw fish and a goat were placed in a flat boat made of wood. Wreaths were draped in between houses, held up by ribbons and wire. The Matriarch's main advisor stood in the centre, listing the healthy, of-age bucks and does selected from the sign-up sheet for the Torthe celebrations. The doe Hylena, with flowers wrapped around her small horns danced in her place, hooves swinging to a melody only she could hear. Kiprencion. Ithelal. Forjden.

Then his own name. Bhearen. They'd caught the tail-end of the speech, missing the first announcements. Another buck, Sylodon, walked up to them when the announcement finished.

"Congratulations on our selection, buck-braethers."

Aren scowled, but Bhearen couldn't stop smiling. He could picture it all now: the river branching off in venous parts, with five off-shoots. Most of the participants would go down the first two on the right, but Bhearen would select the farthest on the left, and Aren would follow.

They'd moor their boat upstream on their part of the river. Water would lap up their legs and between their cloven toes, river debris and weeds clinging to the fur up to the knee. Aren's grey irises would be their usual liquid river, but this time would be specked with moonlight. As usual, he'd grumble about the cold while getting the boat safely tied up: the frost in the air, the water between his thighs, the chills in the intersection of flesh and metal in his head and leg.

A trout would dart through the water, a slice of silver cutting up the moon. Aren's hands would lash out, skimming against the bony ridges of its tail fin, but he wouldn't quite grab it. He'd punch up water in annoyance with a single splash. Bhearen would then teach him, reaching out to position his arm and hips just so.

It would give Bhearen permission to tease him, with a raised brow. "You're not sneaking a second fish for a second lover, are you? That's cheating."

Aren would rub the tender raised skin at the base of his crafted horn as if bashful. "Not like any doe would go for someone with a damaged scent gland. And no. I was just trying to prove I could have your skill with water."

"You don't."

Aren would be aghast, and then Bhearen would be too. Even he couldn't imagine himself as a smooth talker, words always coming out too blunt, rude and blundering as he rehearsed his seduction in his own mind. Back to square one in his fantasy: "I didn't mean it negatively! Only, it's something that needs to be trained. Like your scouting ability! I don't have that."

Bhearen paused in his daydreams, remembering how he had stood in a river much like the one in his mind for hours in the dead of winter. Day after day, month after month, plunging his hands into water after moving targets or nothing, just trying to get used to speed and temperature. His skin would be blooming numb with purple, blue and pink spots and veins, as his Buckathair recorded the details and cheered him on. Be strong for your Doemathair.

Bhearen was pulled out of his fantasy by a shrill scream.

"Everyone, come quick!" Someone was yelling from a side alley off the main square. Bhearen's reflexes kicked in and he dashed away, Aren running behind him. He skidded to a halt at the entrance of the alleyway.

The smell of vomit stung his sinuses and caused bile to rise in his own throat, but it could not cover up the stench of blood. Matri was shivering at the side of the alley, crying into the wooden walls of her house. She must have been sneaking out the back window when she happened upon the traumatic scene.

There were wings on the ground, beside a dumpster. Only, they weren't simple bird wings of feathers. They seemed to pulsate, flesh cut-into shape but seemingly living still. Feathers surrounded it, seemingly plucked out or thrown in a violent shake. Leather-stretched, venous spread—little lines of red hanging around a mucus sheath which breathed wetly over the harder muscle underneath. Blood and ochre perfumed the air with each movement. The living tissue shuddered. How had someone animated it? The only person who could was—

Bhearen vomited.

Beside it was the body of another Capricorn outsider, flat on their stomach. Only, their adaptations on the human form had clearly been three-fold. Their fish tail hung limp, silver scales dull in the light. On their back were two hacked out stumps, blackened with blood. There were signs of a struggle. Skid marks from where their knees had hit the ground and been pushed.

Could picture it now. His Buckathair, experimenting on himself late at night. Manipulating cells in a Petri dish. Growing structures. Drawing diagrams of wings and fins.

Beneath the bloody wings was a message, scrawled in familiar capslock. 'THIS IS A MERCY.'

The Matriarch caught up to him, face as white as parchment. "We found your Buckathair."

About the Author:

Brianna Bullen is a Deakin University PhD creative writing candidate writing about memory in science fiction. She has had work published in journals including LiNQ, Aurealis, Voiceworks, Rabbit, Multiverse: An anthology of international science fiction poetry, and Woolf Pack Zine. She won the 2017 Apollo Bay short story competition and placed second in the 2017 Newcastle Short story competition. Her manuscript was previously a finalist in the 2018 Subbed In Poetry Chapbook competition. In 2018, she was part of Nexus, an Arts Access Victoria collective for artists with mental health recovery lived experience.

THIS IS THE DAWNING
(PART I)

Helena McAuley

It started with the death of Gemini.

She's not a pretty sight, lying broken in a pool of her own blood. It's thickened, coagulated, less like a liquid and more like sticky taffy. Hips shattered, spine broken in at least three different places, her arms and legs at angles unnatural for a human incarnation. Her frizzy, malnourished hair is matted thick with blood, brains, and shards of skull. I won't even talk about the excrement.

What killed her was obviously the blow of her skull hitting the pavement. She'd struck it with force enough to fracture the bone all the way through, causing a rift that split her face from brow to chin, separating her vacant eyes and cutting right through a damned knowing smile.

"I guess now you really are a two-faced bitch," I mutter to her corpse.

A disappointed sigh escapes me as I crouch beside her.

The stark torches of the crime scene investigation render her clothed in light and shadow. I glance up at the overpass from which she'd fallen, sometime in the dead of night, then turn back to her rent face.

"Oh, Gem." I sigh again. "What the hell happened to you?"

I can understand the *tsks* and headshakes of disapproval from the investigators that surround me, unaware of my presence. Gemini's incarnation was nowhere near as old as mine, but unlike me she allowed her physical form to embrace every day of its age. Sagging, wrinkled skin barely clinging to her arms and legs, the lengths of frizzy hair she never bothered to care for, muscles and bones as withered by age as by neglect. In life, her face held a youthfulness despite dry skin and deep furrows. Now in death, that vigour is almost unrecognisable.

A kid in a fancy suit and armed with a notepad approaches the chief investigator with an almost bored and disappointed expression.

"There's nothing up there, boss," he tells her. "No weapons, so signs of a struggle, no blood. Just her other shoe."

The chief investigator almost growls as she strips her hands of their latex gloves. "No identification, either," she says. She gives Gem a cursory glance. "I'd say our Jane Doe was a suicide."

Not Gemini. Not ever. Not because of some deep-seated ideal of morality, or concern of the impact on her so-called loved ones, but because she loved life. She fully embraced every moment, even if that moment was just sitting in front of the television in her cluttered bedsit with a far-too-large box of chocolates. Gemini—the twin, that two-faced bitch—always had one face turned outward and the other turned in— simultaneously facing the material and the spiritual. I've known her through many incarnations, and each is different;

sometimes vain, sometimes passionate. Sometimes, as this one had been, one step shy of being a bloody hermit. But there were two aspects of her that never changed—she would always see both sides, and she always loved life.

I never told her—would never give her the *satisfaction* of telling her—but I think this incarnation had been my favourite so far.

I wonder if she'll choose to incarnate again, before the end.

It's a stupid move on my part with so many humans around—the police, CSI, and morbid lookers-on—but I reach out to touch her, allowing myself to manifest in the process. As a brother to a sister I press my lips to her forehead; ignoring the blood and cold, unyielding flesh. "Return to the stars, Gemini," I whisper to her. "Rest."

Curses and drawn weapons meet my form.

Yeah, pretty stupid.

"Who the hell are you!" the kid with the fancy suit shrieks. "Where the hell did you *come from!*"

I don't bother to look up at them as I remove my hand from Gem's broken face and give them a dismissive wave. *"Forget,"* I command, and let the manifestation drop. The two look at their suddenly drawn firearms at first with shock, then confusion, then they finally holster them with an air of embarrassment.

I walk through the barriers and growing crowds. Not just past them, *through* them; the press of bodies and tangible objects as meaningless to me as the alarmed squabbling that proceeds from the kid and his boss. They don't know what they have—wouldn't be able to understand the enormity of the implications even if I bothered to explain. This wasn't accident, or suicide, or even an ordinary act of murder.

This was an act of war.

A war that, if not won, will shatter the foundations of their only concept of reality.

I have to find a way to win it, as much for my own sake as for theirs.

The new Age is dawning. I've felt it coming for a while now; a slow building of tension and urgency in my being, two hundred years in its coming. But now, as I walk through streets still dark but awakening with their first taste of the morn's sun, I can feel it spill over. Like a cup too full. The delicate inaction of the previous centuries is a path no longer open to me, not only because of the sudden urgency of the situation, but because nothing less is physically possible anymore. My mind races, unable to be stemmed by my usual methods. My limbs are tense with the need for *action.*

Fine then. Have it your way. I manifest and allow this body to become grounded to the material world, to feel the sudden weight of gravity pulling at my bones, the firm resistance of the concrete pushing up at my feet, the wall of air striking my body, then yielding and sliding across my skin.

I should probably try to conserve my energy; for what is to come.

I have been incarnate every day of this Age—a feat not attempted by any of my fellows, not even Pisces, the ruler of this Age, head as much among the stars as it is on the ground, even when incarnate.

There are benefits to remaining incarnate for so long; the physical body becomes just another *thing*, entirely subject to your will. But the millennia take a toll on the mind. In the midst of the building tension of the Dawning, that toll is more again—I can feel it threatening to tear me apart. I need to rest. But I can't—not now. Not until the job is done.

The twists and turns of the streets and alleys lead me to

THIS IS THE DAWNING (PART I)

Dante's Café. I, like my fellows, don't need food or drink the way humans do, but indulgence comes in differing levels. You could almost say this place is one of my 'haunts'. I sit at the counter and order a strong coffee, the stimulation of the caffeine bringing artificial life to this physical form.

I can't get the image of Gemini out of my mind. Bloody and broken, a Mona Lisa smile, infuriating in its knowingness. What did she know? What did she see before the end? What was the last thing that passed through her mind? Well, besides the pavement, at least.

I rub at my face, feeling the coarse grit of unattended stubble, and release a sigh verging on a growl. Gem, what the hell *happened* to you?

I have my suspicions. I guess it's time I spoke with Pisces.

I do own a phone—an item required to navigate the modern world—but this is a conversation not to be overheard by telecommunication lines. There is no change to my outward appearance, no slowing of my hands turning the pages of the unread newspaper before me, or lifting the coffee to my lips, no dampening of the awareness of my surroundings. But my mind is elsewhere.

I reach out.

Gemini is dead.

What.? I hear the groggy response. *Capricorn, is this a joke? You're disturbing me in the middle of my morning yoga.*

No joke. I saw the body myself.

There's a pause, but not a silence. I *feel* as much as *hear* the shifting, the internal debate.

Then Gemini will incarnate again, and we will still be the Twelve.

I don't think so, Pi.

But the Dawning!

And that is exactly what I think this is about.

Another pause, more deliberate this time. An alertness, a stilling.

It was Sagittarius, I add.

The stillness deepens. *You can't know that.*

I do, Pi. I do know it. The Twelve contend for supremacy at the time of the Dawning, but now the Twelve are only eleven. Sagittarius is the greatest malcontent, the one who doesn't want the Ages to follow their proper order. Why wait for the battle? Why not pick us off before allegiances can be formed? The fewer of us there are, the fewer required for consensus. The fewer of us to dominate.

So what? Gemini will re-incarnate—

Not this time.

Why not?

I turn the page of the newspaper as I reply. *The Dawning has already begun. Are you telling me you haven't felt it? There'll be no more incarnations. Not until this is resolved.*

Pisces withdraws, only slightly, but I feel her trepidation and anxiety. I sip at my coffee and let it burn my tongue.

Cap, you're scaring me.

We need to start to bring the others into line.

No, Cap. You're scaring me because you have this so well thought out. You don't know what happened, you can't *know what happened! And no one ever knows which way Gemini is going to swing.*

Hesitation, uncertainty, and fear.

It almost sounds like you're trying to frame Sagittarius.

I DID NOT KILL GEMINI!

Rage explodes from me, tensing my muscles, tightening my jaw, releasing a deep rumble from the earth. The few humans attending the café in the early morning light let out gasps and cries of shock as the ground trembles; cutlery and crockery tinkle against each other, and the lights flicker.

Capricorn! Calm down!

The tremors subside as fury is quickly replaced by alarm. That was stupid. *Stupid.* I stand and throw coins enough on the counter to pay for the unfinished coffee, then swiftly leave the café. It's the damn Dawning, its power flowing through me, the state of uncertainty in the cosmos. I can't allow it to get the better of me a second time.

Capricorn. Pisces' voice is tender. *How long have you been incarnate?*

Two-thousand-nine-hundred-and-seventy-three years.

Cap! That's more than an Age!

I don't respond to that, I just let the ignominy burn through me.

Capricorn, I know this is the Dawning, but . . . Hesitation again. *Maybe you should dis-incarnate.*

No.

You need to rest! The burden of incarnation—

Is something I can handle. I don't need a lecture. I need allies. *I can rest later. This is more important.*

Pisces' disapproval is almost tangible as I walk through the now sunlit streets. The day has begun, and the humans are waking to it. The world is filling with sounds and smells unknown to the night.

I feel, more than hear, the sigh. *Okay. Remember that I am here for you. What do you need me to do?*

The proper order must be maintained. My tone is hard enough to be a command. *Entreat, beg, and threaten anyone you can. And let me know who you get.*

What are you going to do?

I look over the street, at the growing passage of commuters, joggers, and rabble. The night was late, and the day will be long. Sleep is not required, but rest . . . That is another matter.

Still, I unmanifest and melt into the streets.

Capricorn?
The answer should have been obvious.
I'm going to find Aquarius.

To be continued in the next edition of the Zodiac Series . . .

About the Author:

Helena McAuley loves trees and hates paper. That is why, when she finds paper, she must constantly desecrate it with her "writing".
Lover of whisky, social justice, and the Oxford Comma, McAuley's aim for her writing is to produce memorable characters and enjoyable stories that lure the unsuspecting reader into introspective thought.

A former student of archaeology and anthropology, McAuley has been published in the Williamstown Writers anthology 'On the Edge'; the complaints section of her local newspaper; and her mother's bi-annual letters home to family.

This is the Dawning *is a serialised debut that will be published throughout the ASF Zodiac series. So if you want to know what Capricorn does next—har har—you have to read Aquarius. She can be found twit-ing, insta-ing, and occasionally facebooked under the handle @thathmc*

No goats or fish were harmed during the making of this anthology.

ABOUT AUSSIE SPECULATIVE FICTION

Aussie Speculative Fiction is a recently established group which was created to support and promote Australian speculative fiction writers.
Check out our links:
www.facebook.com/aussiespeculativefiction
www.twitter.com/aussiefiction
www.aussiespeculativefiction.com
www.books2read.com/rl/asf

ABOUT DEADSET PRESS

Deadset Press is the publishing imprint of Aussie Speculative Fiction - a community aimed at supporting Australian and Kiwi authors. You can learn more at:

www.aussiespeculativefiction.com

ALSO BY DEADSET PRESS

Annual Anthologies

Drowned Earth